Charlotte Lexington:
DUNGEON OF UNKNOWN DOOM

JULIA GAO

LITTLE CREEK PRESS®
AND BOOK DESIGN
MINERAL POINT, WISCONSIN

Copyright © 2022 by Julia Gao

All rights reserved. No part of this publication may be reproduced, distributed, or transmitted in any form or by any means, including photocopying, recording, digital scanning, or other electronic or mechanical methods, without the prior written permission of the publisher, except in the case of brief quotations embodied in critical reviews and certain other noncommercial uses permitted by copyright law. For permission requests or other information, please send correspondence to the following address:

Little Creek Press
5341 Sunny Ridge Road
Mineral Point, WI 53565

ORDERING INFORMATION
Quantity sales. Special discounts are available on quantity purchases by corporations, associations, and others. For details, contact info@littlecreekpress.com

Orders by US trade bookstores and wholesalers.
Please contact Little Creek Press or Ingram for details.

Printed in the United States of America

Cataloging-in-Publication Data
Names: Gao, Julia, author
Title: Charlotte Lexington: Dungeon of Unknown Doom / Julia Gao
Description: Mineral Point, WI; Little Creek Press, 2022
Identifiers: LCCN: 2022918128 | ISBN: 978-1-955656-33-7
Subjects: FICTION / Fantasy / Action & Adventure

Book design by Little Creek Press

Cover:
Mountains: shutterstock_145799588
Castle and dragon: shutterstock_2066621858

Dedicated to J.K. Rowling,
Rick Riordan, J.R.R. Tolkien,
and all the amazing
authors in the
world.

Table of Contents

Preface 7

ONE: Country Club Greens 11

TWO: Professor Austin. 27

THREE: Hermes Plaza. 37

FOUR: Mountain View School of Magic. 49

FIVE: The Entrance Exams 59

SIX: Friends and Foes 69

SEVEN: The Dungeon of Unknown Doom 81

EIGHT: Tests and Truths 89

NINE: Penelope Brown 97

TEN: Trouble 111

ELEVEN: Bit by Bit 125

TWELVE: Into the Dungeon. 137

THIRTEEN: Home 177

Acknowledgments 191

About the Author 192

Preface

Dear Reader,

Thank you for picking up this book. Many people helped me with this book, but I would give most of my thanks to the wonderful author, J.K. Rowling. She has inspired me to continue writing and she changed the way I look at the world. I was especially impressed about how she was able to connect reality and her own fantasy world so well.

In the spring semester of 2019, my classmates and I campaigned to invite J.K. Rowling to pay a visit to Black Rock Elementary School. Over a one-month campaign, we collected around 900 signatures from our fellow students, their parents, and teachers. In the package I sent her, I included my book, pictures of the beautiful snowcapped Rocky Mountains, and an offer from a friend to stay in his chalet, which has a incredible view of Longs Peak and is very close to the National Park. My teammates suggested decorating the package box with our welcoming photos and our school logo before sending it out.

This reminds me of the dedication of a book series, The Land of Stories, which I enjoyed. Chris Colfer said that he had spent so much of his childhood waiting for his Hogwarts letter. This is my story, too.

My dad's friend, a literature professor named, Randy McCrain, has talked to me occasionally about the history of fantasy stories and the authors at Oxford University, such as C.S. Lewis and J.R.R Tolkien. This led me to explore a diversity of books and authors.

My district Gifted and Talented teacher, Mrs. Kristin Pierce, read my book, helped edit my book, and also made a long reading list for me. I'd like to mention the Percy Jackson series for their humorous approach to writing. I appreciate the way Rick Riordan mixed mythology with the life of an average middle schooler.

I did a lot of research to make names of the characters meaningful. For example, Professor Ventum and Professor Iris are based on Latin words. Others, like Sam, are based on stars and constellations. I also used names from famous book characters like Penelope, while other names have come from Greek mythology, like Athena, or the Bible. J.K. Rowling had also used this technique, and I like some of the names that had come out, and most of them fit perfectly in a few ways. If you do some research you will see that most of them have a meaning that suits the character. This has helped me understand etymology better and apply it to my own writing.

I also do believe I should say thank you to my many teachers who made me love reading and writing. I remember a card that I received from my third-grade teacher, Ms. Crampsey, and she asked me to remember her when I become famous. So, no worries, I have remembered, and I would like to mention you right now.

And now, I thank you again, Reader. Please enjoy this book, and I will be ready to write the next one.

Yours sincerely,

Julia Gao
Boulder, Colorado

ONE

Country Club Greens

It was an ordinary early August day in Boulder, Colorado. Eight-year-old Charlotte Lexington sat on her front porch in her neighborhood, Country Club Greens, watching her dog, Jelly, roll on the grass.

There are a variety of ways to describe Charlotte, and she was known for a variety of different things.

She's smart, which would rather be an understatement, but relatively true, nonetheless. She was also an orphan; both her parents died in a car crash when she was two. She now lived alone with her single, introverted uncle, Mr. Lexington, in Boulder, Colorado.

Her uncle was a meteorologist, and also a professor at Princeton University. This year, they had moved to Colorado from New Jersey so her uncle could study the mysterious wildfires happening in the national park with increasing frequency. It was just barely Charlotte's third month here.

Colorado was prone to wildfires, but this was something separate, on a whole other level. It seemed now that every month there would be another fire, and they were extremely ferocious. Most of them seemed to originate from the mountains, but they would spread down from the national park, occasionally endangering even the urban residential areas. The fires have plagued parts of Longmont, Allenspark, Louisville, Superior, and all the surrounding towns. It was most peculiar.

Mr. Lexington now worked with scientists at the University of Colorado at Boulder, researching the mysterious origins of these catastrophic wildfires. He was a dapper and respectable man, but his defining characteristic was his impeccable neatness and the precision with which he handled everything.

One time, he and Charlotte were baking cupcakes. He taught Charlotte to level the measuring cup three times before adding each ingredient. And it was all very well for the sugar and flour, but he also insisted on doing the same for "half a teaspoon of salt."

Her uncle did not tolerate uncleanliness and mess. Charlotte had not had a play date since she was six. She had invited her preschool friend to her house, and after her friend left, she and her uncle restacked every toy, vacuumed every room, and wiped every surface. After the tiring cleaning procedure, she had rather lost her enthusiasm for play dates.

Meanwhile, Charlotte was also looking for a new school near her new home. She had toured multiple elementary schools in the district already with her uncle, but she could not decide which one to go to. All of them felt unfamiliar to her in this new place, although her extraordinary brains could've gotten her anywhere with ease. Her uncle constantly asked which school she'd like to enroll in, but she still didn't know. It was already early August, and time was running out.

The grass at her feet was emerald green. Their lawn stretched out to a small green pond. Reeds danced in the wind, and dragonflies whistled through the air. A large maple tree cast a cool shadow over the porch. It seemed like perfect paradise.

However, if you stood up, you could see the smoke billowing like great clouds across the houses, coming from the Rocky Mountains. The faint scent of smoke lingered in the air, and flakes of ash coated the nearby shrubs and bushes.

Charlotte shook these thoughts out of her mind and joined Jelly, flopping down on the grass.

By some coincidence, at precisely the same moment she laid her head down, Mr. Lexington walked out.

He spotted her. "Charlotte, get up!" her uncle told her. "It's so difficult to clean grass stains. It took me two-point-five ounces of detergent last time and used up all my stain remover!

"I need to run to the supermarket." Mr. Lexington jingled his keys. "I forgot the seasoning for the steak. Also, didn't you say you needed pencils?"

Charlotte sat up and walked back to the porch.

"Yeah," Charlotte shrugged. "I guess."

"Okay then," Mr. Lexington said. "I'll get a dozen. Right now it is six. I shall be back in fifteen minutes. Would you mind firing up the grill for me at six-twelve?"

"Sure, I can do that," she said, carrying Jelly through the door.

Charlotte set Jelly down and glanced around the house. It was tidy like always. She turned on the grill in the backyard on time, then she sidled about the house, looking for something to do. She eventually occupied herself with a small puzzle, which she made sure to conceal in her closet. Charlotte was almost certain that Mr. Lexington would have a seizure if he laid eyes on the scattered pieces all over the floor.

A quarter of an hour later, Mr. Lexington returned.

"Here are your pencils," he said, handing a bright orange packet to her.

"Thanks," Charlotte said, taking them.

"Grill time!" he held up the seasoning bottle and shook it. Charlotte followed him into the kitchen, where he had sprinkled the steak with exactly a quarter cup of seasoning, then as always, he patted it down on both sides for thirty seconds.

Charlotte checked on the grill, which was hot, and Mr. Lexington arrived shortly with the steak. He set them on the grill, and Jelly ran over as if he wanted steak too.

"No, Jelly!" Charlotte laughed. "No human food for you. But some dog food is due around now."

Mr. Lexington spent this time waiting patiently beside the grill, checking the steak temperature in intervals of five minutes, until it was exactly 125 degrees, medium rare.

It was indeed very tasty. As they savored the juicy steak, Mr. Lexington asked, "Charlotte, have you decided on a school yet?"

Charlotte looked up and shook her head.

"I can't decide," she told him.

"How about we stick with Oakland Elementary, the public school? I think the teachers there are all very nice, and of course, the curriculum is quite good there, I reviewed it when we toured the school. They even scored 4.7 stars on the review website."

"But it is so different from my old school!" Charlotte wiped her mouth with a napkin and took a sip of water, looking up pleadingly at Mr. Lexington. "I want to go to a private school! I thought you said I could choose Timber Creek instead! The curriculum at Oakland Elementary is far too easy, how are they still doing arithmetic in fourth grade? That is so boring."

"Of course, Charlotte, I know you are incredibly bright. However, since we just moved here, I think you should take some time to socialize and make some friends at school instead of immediately immersing yourself in the most difficult curriculum available. Just take one year in public school perhaps, and make some connections. If you don't like it, we can transfer you to Timber Creek next year. And if you think it's too easy, we can accelerate you a bit, maybe even skip a grade, how about that?" added Mr. Lexington consolingly.

"But that's an entire year wasted!" said Charlotte in distress.

"Did you like Oakland when we toured it?" Mr. Lexington inquired.

"It was ok, I liked the facility, people looked welcoming, I guess. But still, the curriculum there is too simple for me, I don't like it... I mean, both are not optimal, Timber Creek has a very limited course selection as well, but at least for the core subjects, they are more advanced."

"Charlotte," Mr. Lexington said slowly. "I know you are incredibly intelligent. You can do algebra at eight, almost nine, and you read Shakespeare and classics reserved for middle and high school students! You speak multiple languages and have many, many talents! You are the sharpest kid I've ever met, there's no denying it. I understand that, but I also want you to make friends, and socialize a bit! If you want to accelerate yourself, you can come back in the evenings and I can help you work on some harder questions. I can even take you to my lab on the weekends, how would you like that? But, my advice is, go to Oakland this one year, alright?"

Charlotte lowered her eyes to her plate grudgingly and grunted,

"Fine, I'll think about it. I could go to a boarding school too, as long as it's a good one with a competitive curriculum. If you can find one like that, I'll go and you can stay focused on your research for the wildfire."

"That's very considerate, thank you," Mr. Lexington said. "I'll see about the boarding school, but I doubt I'll find any around here for you, because you're too young. But please choose well, you only have a few weeks left!"

"I know, uncle," Charlotte responded, digging back into her food. "By the way, did you find anything on the wildfires?"

"We have a lead," her uncle answered. "Last week we did some field research. A few years ago, all the pine trees in the national park underwent a severe pine beetle infestation. Thousands of trees died and fell. As it's been so dry and hot these years, and high winds up to 120 miles per hour have been documented a few times. They could've easily caught fire and subsequently spread. But, it still does not explain the speed with which they spread and how they recurred over and over again in such close succession, even in winter!"

"It's so strange!" said Charlotte in awe. "Well, good luck uncle! Let me know if you find anything. I really want all the people to be safe."

After dinner, Charlotte stood up and looked around the house. She was out of things to do. She wanted to call Natasha, one of her old friends from New Jersey.

Charlotte pulled out her phone and dialed Natasha on the way up the stairs. She picked up within a millisecond.

"Charlotte!" she exclaimed.

"Hi Nat," responded Charlotte.

"How are you?" she immediately asked. "Are you ok? How's Colorado?"

"Not bad," said Charlotte. "But I miss you, and I miss home very much. I think the wildfires are ruining this whole experience for me. Please, fill me in on what's happening back there."

After fifteen minutes on the phone with Natasha, Charlotte hung up, feeling even more homesick than before. She spent the rest of the evening reading *Call of the Wild* by Jack London. She sat on the couch, deep in her reading with a pencil tucked behind her ear. Her uncle sat at the dinner table, researching and writing papers on his laptop. Light jazz played from the radio, and only two lamps were on. They cast a soft, warm glow over the entire living room. It was peaceful.

Just before bedtime, her uncle stood up and turned on the TV. It was the evening news.

At once, the newscaster's voice punctured the silence, listing the fatalities, injuries, and destroyed territories of the day. The screen showed ragged people, carrying children, leading the elderly, all in great despair.

"And today, the sixth wildfire in Colorado this year spreads from Estes Park all the way down to Louisville. James Token is in Boulder, Colorado, with the newest information. James, what's it like for the residents of this area as historic wildfires endanger not only the national park but also residential areas?"

A lady came up to the screen, her matted hair sticking to her face, which was black with soot. She clutched a great big pile of blankets and clothes, and a wailing baby was perched on top of all this. Her shoulders slumped forwards in exhaustion.

The camera zoomed out and displayed the hundreds of people trekking towards the shelter, the crowd winding along the road like a terrible black snake.

A baby's cries were heard on the broadcast as the camera focused on the mountains, which were so beautiful months prior, but now there was no green patches of trees, it was all a pitiful charcoal black...

"Please stop it!" Charlotte stood up in distress and grabbed the pencil from behind her ear. She flinched as a few brilliant white sparks shot out of the TV with a resounding *bang!* Then she saw the TV had disappeared, leaving nothing behind!

"Oh goodness!" her uncle said aloud.

"What?" Charlotte said, as she turned around frantically, searching for the missing TV. She looked at her uncle, he was on his feet too, watching Charlotte with a curious expression.

"Uncle?" Charlotte asked uncertainly. "What just happened?"

Mr. Lexington walked over to Charlotte collectedly. He looked her in the eyes and placed his hands on each of her shoulders.

"Uh, Charlotte, don't worry. I think it was a power outage due to the wildfires. The high voltage could've caused an overload. It'll be alright in the morning, there's nothing to worry about, now. It's bedtime, Charlotte, alright?"

Charlotte nodded, still in shock.

Her uncle sent her up to bed, tucked her in, and assured her it was just a power outage and she shouldn't be concerned. The power grid should be back on very soon. Charlotte nodded and listened, but she knew, she knew that power outages don't make your TV disappear into thin air. She was smart enough to see that her bedroom light, the living room lamp, and the microwave light were still on. She knew something extraordinary was happening.

She tossed and turned in bed, still amazed and shocked, and very curious. After nearly an hour of restlessness, she began to slowly doze off. In her dreams, she kept revisiting the images of the poor people displaced by the fire. They flashed through her mind, one by one. Suddenly, her dreams became something different.

Around her, all was dark except for a pearly white silhouette of a person that drifted towards her from the distance. As it approached, its white light blinded Charlotte, but Charlotte could make out that it was a woman.

As the woman approached, Charlotte observed that she had long, wavy hair that reached her waist, and soft brown eyes similar to Charlotte's. She hesitated a moment, and then asked, "Mom?" The ghost stopped a few feet away from Charlotte, and nodded serenely.

"Charlotte," the ghost whispered. Its face was indistinguishable, smoky and unclear, but the voice aroused something deep in Charlotte. A memory from long ago, that she didn't even know she had.

"Mom!" Charlotte whispered again, unable to move, seemingly paralyzed, in deep awe. "This can't be true!"

"Charlotte, I have come to warn you, your life is about to change."

"What, why?" Charlotte asked, still focusing on the fact that she was speaking, actually speaking, to her mother, staring entranced at the figure's face, trying to distinguish her looks.

"I cannot stay long. But you know the people need your help. You can help them."

"I don't understand," Charlotte said, unfocused. This all seemed insignificant to her, all that was important was that her mother was here.

"Charlotte, listen, listen! The people need your help!"

"I want to, but how?" Charlotte finally asked, trying to memorize the sound of her mother's voice.

"You will discover very soon," her mother replied. "But it will be difficult and dangerous. I am warning you now, but it is your destiny."

"What do you mean?" asked Charlotte hurriedly.

"You are destined to help them, but it will be dangerous, so all I can say is good luck, Charlotte. And please, stay safe, take care, Charlotte, dear…"

Then slowly, the ghostly form of Olivia Lexington drifted backwards, back into the darkness…

"Mom, mom, mom…"

Charlotte woke with a start. She blinked twice and glanced over at the alarm clock on her bedside table. It was almost six. She yawned and sat up, then walked over to the window.

Dawn was breaking outside, a fiery orange glow emanating from behind the jagged mountains, spreading across the horizon. The sky transitioned from red to a light blue, and it was a simply cloudless morning. The sun itself was starting to peek out behind the cliffs now, the golden epicenter of all the light, a vibrant ball that blazed itself into her eyelids. It was perfectly framed between two old cottonwood trees, shimmering off their canopies. Charlotte blinked. A light breeze made the leaves on the cottonwoods dance and sing, and drops of dew glistened on the windowsill. It was all so quiet and peaceful, but Charlotte kept dwelling on her dream.

Was that really her mother? And what did her words mean? Of course, Charlotte would like to help the suffering people, but how could she?

As she continued to stare out at the beautiful sunrise, she suddenly noticed a great large dot come into view on the horizon. Its silhouette looked like a magnificent bird, maybe a bald eagle?

As it soared ever closer, Charlotte saw the warm light reflecting off its glossy wings. It circled and began to dive, and before Charlotte even comprehended what was happening, the bird flew straight at the window.

Instinctively, Charlotte raised her arms to shield her face and ducked down. "What on earth?"

Charlotte waited in anticipation and with bated breath, but there was crash, no *crunch* of breaking window. When Charlotte chanced a glance up, she saw the bird perched on her desk, inside of her room, but the window was still intact, and closed!

The bird—a handsome and very large pigeon—was looking straight at her, its golden eyes boring into hers. A pebble was in his beak, its pristine silver feathers fluttering in the wind.

"A pigeon," Charlotte mused, still flabbergasted at how it got in. "You here for me?" The pigeon seemed to nod, bobbing its serene neck up and down thrice.

"How did you get in here?"

The pigeon cocked its head to either way in a mischievous sort of way, and stuck out a leg.

There was a golden piece of parchment stuck to the pigeon's leg in a little leather pouch. Charlotte frowned. What was this? A pigeon had come to deliver a letter to her?

"Nobody uses pigeons for mail anymore! They did in World War II, but now we have email..."

Carefully, she reached out and removed the letter from the pigeon's leg. It was in faded gold parchment, stamped with a coat of arms bearing a large, silver *W*.

Wands surrounded the *W*. One on top of the *W*, one underneath, and one on each side. The wands were connected with ivy, a poisonous color of green.

She unrolled it to find a long letter, made with a neat, black script, it read:

Dear Charlotte Lexington,

Greetings! We are pleased to inform you that you are a witch of magical descent, and therefore you have been admitted to Mountain View School of Magic.

Though it may sound bizarre, we can guarantee that you possess magical blood and magical abilities. These abilities may be honed, controlled, and enlarged at Mountain View School of Magic.

To prove to and introduce you to the magical world, on the 23rd of August, we shall send Professor Athena Austin of Mountain View School to visit your abode. She will make clear all precautions and give you directions or a guide to Hermes Plaza, where you may find and purchase necessary equipment and textbooks to aid you in your academic pursuits here at school.

As a brief of your semester schedule, you will start school on the 23rd of August and end on June 14th the following year. As Mountain View is a boarding school, you will stay in the dorms except for all breaks longer than three days. In such cases, students generally prefer to return to visit home. Going is optional, however, and staying at school is also a choice. Your semester exams will be held in the last week of your school year, and grades will be delivered to your dormitories before your departure for the summer.

We also would like to make clear that all information regarding Mountain View School of Magic must be kept confidential to anyone who is not a witch or wizard.

Thank you, and please enjoy the rest of your vacation!

Sincerely,
Helios Watonburn
The Headmaster, Mountain View School of Magic

    Charlotte gasped and read it again and again.
    She bit her lip. Then she shook her head. What was wrong with her? It must be a trick! How could she possibly believe something as outrageous as this so quickly?

"I suppose it's some weird trick. No one uses pigeons for mail anymore, and where on earth would there be wizards and witches? They don't live underground or something, do they? If they were walking on the street and building magical buildings, wouldn't we know what's going on?"

Now she was making sense. She folded the letter.

"Though, this seems real. I have a good feeling about it. Let's just wait for Professor Austin then."

What did she just say?

But it was true, despite all of this being very strange, something more peculiar stirred inside her. A feeling, like she knew it was true. Despite never having heard a thing about any of this—wizards, witches, magical boarding schools—she decided over logic to believe. There must be a reason. Could it be?

She turned to check her calendar. "August 23rd is my birthday! You know, if this is real, it'll be a nice present! But I'm not telling anyone about it in case it isn't true. It could just be a weird prank. Someone caught a pigeon and then wrote a letter about wizards and made up some names and told the pigeon to...?"

She paused, her brain whirring.

"Okay, how *does* the pigeon know what to do?"

She rolled up the letter and found a piece of paper on her desk. It wasn't the same golden parchment they used, but Charlotte thought it would have to do.

She wrote down in her neatest handwriting:

Dear Professor Watonburn,

Are you sure this isn't all made up? I hope this is not some sort of prank. I'm sure you understand such information is highly implausible. I mean, where is Mountain View? Who exactly are you?

Sincerely,
Charlotte Lexington

She tied it back onto the pigeon's leg and sent it out through the window.

"Bye!" she called after it, as it spread its wings and soared away across the velvety blue sky, a spot of grey in a sea of cerulean.

Settling down in her room, she looked at the letter again.

"It should be real. Who would put so much effort into pulling a prank, catching and training pigeons, writing letters, and sending them to my house?" she said to herself.

Suddenly, a spark ignited in her brain, and she opened the door and bolted downstairs.

She stomped to the kitchen counter, flung open a cabinet door, chose a mug, and started making hot chocolate.

Charlotte supposed she had been a little too loud, because her uncle came out from his room a few moments later.

"Did I disturb you?" Charlotte asked apologetically.

"A little," he responded. "It's ok, I should be up by now too."

Then, he saw the piece of golden parchment in Charlotte's free hand.

"What's that?"

"Uncle..." Charlotte took a deep breath. "I got an invitation, an acceptance letter, to a boarding school, just like we discussed last night!"

Her uncle tilted his head curiously, smiling a little. "Wow, but what do you mean? You didn't even go outside last night!"

Slowly, gingerly, Charlotte raised her hand and held out the delicately rolled up parchment, and Mr. Lexington stared at the coat of arms.

"Whose arms are these?" he asked.

"You'll know when you read it," Charlotte replied. "I can hardly believe it, but I'm so excited!"

Mr. Lexington took the piece of parchment and unrolled it. He lowered his eyes and began reading, his eyebrows near his hairline, his eyes squinted, radiating disbelief.

When he finished, he wouldn't look at Charlotte. He eventually asked, "How'd this get to you anyway?"

As Charlotte opened her mouth, a second pigeon, this one white, swooped in through the open window. He folded his wings and settled daintily on the couch, hopped, and held out a leg.

Charlotte bent down to retrieve the letter, and Mr. Lexington's eyes narrowed sharply.

"Not a bird?"

"Yeah," Charlotte said, laughing. "I woke up, and I was watching the beautiful sunrise outside, and a pigeon starts to fly straight at my window! And the most amazing part is, it passed clean through the glass without breaking it at all! Uncle, uncle, this has to be magic right?"

Mr. Lexington smiled. "That does sound very interesting, Charlotte! It may just be."

"May I have the first letter please, uncle?"

Mr. Lexington handed it to her. "What does the second one say?"

Charlotte took the letter from Mr. Lexington and she unrolled the next piece of golden parchment. It read:

Dear Charlotte Lexington,

I can assure you that everything described in the letter is true and very credible. Mountain View is located on the side of Longs Peak, but we cannot give out the exact information until you arrive. I am Helios Phineas Watonburn, the Headmaster. I was educated here and spent 58 years teaching charms at Mountain View prior to assuming my current post. As stated, please await Professor Austin on the 23rd of August. She will answer any questions you may have and help you adjust to the magical world. And yes, I'm sure she will indeed come, and I can promise you it's all real. I understand your confusion, but you will see in due course.

Sincerely,
Helios Watonburn
The Headmaster of Mountain View School of Magic

"So it's true..." Charlotte said. "I just asked Professor Watonburn about the validity of the letter, and the boarding school, because you know, magic."

Mr. Lexington nodded, looking at Charlotte with a mysterious knowingness in his eyes.

"Charlotte, I understand everything that is going on. If you choose this school—and of course, if it exists—you can go there. The most important thing is that, of course, you like it and it engages you in your education. But I have to meet some of the staff, read something about the curriculum, and know exactly where this school is, just in case. I also need to make sure the environment is safe for you, because safety is the most important thing, alright? Other than that, I think this school sounds like a good fit for you."

Charlotte nodded.

"Also, are you not concerned about the curriculum anymore?"

Charlotte grinned. "There's just a feeling inside me that this is where I belong. And maybe I should take a year to socialize and make friends there!"

Her uncle laughed.

"That's wonderful, Charlotte. I'll just need to check a few things with this Professor Austin on August 23rd, and then you can go! Because I'm sure that you know what you did last night was magic, and science cannot explain it! Did you piece it together yourself as well?"

Charlotte nodded.

"You are very smart indeed! Oh, you wanted hot chocolate?" he asked finally, looking at the packet Charlotte clutched in her hand.

Charlotte nodded, and Mr. Lexington helped her warm exactly one and a half cups of milk.

"Thanks. I'll be in my room, uncle," Charlotte told him when a mug of hot, frothy chocolate was in her hand.

Charlotte headed into her room and sipped her hot chocolate.

Besides the burning feeling in her gut, she could also look at the facts.

Unless it was a wizard, who could be in possession of not one but two pigeons, both trained to deliver letters? Even if the sender was but her next-door neighbor, the response was unusually quick.

And the way the pigeon just flew through the glass! That had to be magic! And the TV, too. These were real examples that cannot possibly be ignored.

Suddenly, she couldn't wait! To think of going away for so long to learn something so amazing! Magic! What would she do? Turn people into toadstools? Learn to mind-control people? Learn to duel with spells?

But being sensible, she wanted to test it one last time to make sure. She took a deep breath, set the hot chocolate mug in front of her, and imagined it flying. She wasn't sure if this was the correct way to perform spells or if it would work, but she had to try. Her hands clenched on the tabletop, she stared hard at the blue patterns on the mug, and she muttered under her breath, *"Fly! Fly! Fly!"*

It took a while. Telling herself to concentrate, she returned to chanting "Fly! Fly! Fly!" Her eyes bored into the side of the ceramic mug, sweat beaded up on her forehead, and all her muscles tensed. Suddenly, the mug gave a jolt. Swallowing, Charlotte willed it to move more. As if held up by an invisible hand, slowly, the mug rose unsteadily into the air and circled a few inches above the desktop. Then it dropped. Charlotte lunged and caught it in her hands, then took a warm sip of the frothy contents.

It was true. She was a witch. There was no way anyone could come to a different conclusion after this last experiment.

She walked to her calendar. In blue, she circled August 23rd. Then in red, she circled August 24th.

And so, she waited.

TWO

Professor Austin

It was four in the morning on the 23rd. Charlotte couldn't sleep. Could this all be true?

For the past few weeks, Charlotte had been in incredulous indecision. She had convinced herself she was a witch, for unless her eyes were playing tricks on her, she saw the mug float in the air.

Even part of Charlotte didn't believe this. But it all came down to today. Today, all her questions would be answered. Will this Professor Austin come or not?

It had surely been a very interesting few days. On Thursday evening, her uncle had decided to teach her to bake banana bread. After he had carefully leveled out the flour and added it, Charlotte had had a brilliant idea.

She had taken the salt shaker and unscrewed the lid. Then, she dumped the lot in the bowl.

"What are you doing?" her uncle had cried.

"I—I'm so sorry!" Charlotte then responded, trying to act innocent, telling her uncle she thought it was sugar.

When her uncle had left, a little frustrated, she closed her eyes and willed the salt to disappear. She chanted her wish under her breath five times, and when she opened her eyes—

The salt in the bowl had gone, and the shaker on the counter was magically full. Exuberant, Charlotte had finished the recipe alone, baked it, and presented it to Mr. Lexington.

It was with extreme doubt and hesitancy that Mr. Lexington took a slice. But when he bit into it, Charlotte could see the sudden surprise in his expression.

Grinning, Charlotte had explained her small experiment to him. Mr. Lexington was amazed, and even he could not find a flaw in her method. Charlotte had made sure to present her case carefully, following all the steps of the scientific method that her uncle had taught her.

Charlotte had gone around, experimenting with her magic powers. When she had dropped a plate on accident on Wednesday morning, she chanted *"clean it up!"* under her breath, and the shards had flown themselves into the trash can. Her uncle was certainly most delighted at this.

Eventually, she got up. Her stomach was bubbling with excitement and nervousness.

She picked up the letter again.

It can't be real.

It might be real, though.

But I mean, who's heard of a wizard school?

No, it is real. Professor Watonburn said it's confidential, so no one knows. She'll show up.

No, she won't. It's a prank.

No! It is real!

Doesn't it sound a little like Harry Potter?

Honestly, why couldn't it be real?

Why would it be real whatsoever then?

Thoughts sped across Charlotte's mind like rockets, contradicting each other. Finally, she decided to make breakfast, because who knows how early Professor Austin will come?

Down in the kitchen, she found a loaf of bread from the fridge. She spread peanut butter on a slice and drizzled honey over it, her preferred breakfast. She poured some milk from the jug and sat down. She didn't have much of an appetite. She forced herself to swallow some food and washed it down with the milk.

She washed the plate and the mug before sitting down on the couch. She figured it wouldn't disturb Mr. Lexington too much if she watched some TV. She flipped through the channels.

She stopped at the cartoon channel, but decided it was too childish for someone who was leaving for boarding school to learn magic; next was a politics channel, but she found it was too hard to understand; she made a stop by the nature channel, but felt she wasn't interested at the moment; she turned down the news channel after an exhaustive report on all the damage caused by the wildfires in Colorado that year.

She didn't feel like watching TV anymore. She opened the backdoor for some fresh air, but as she looked up, the sky was clouded with sheets of dark smoke and ash. She felt sick almost immediately, and she turned right back inside. She didn't feel like doing anything.

Jelly toddled over as she closed the door. Jelly's eyes were half-closed; he must've just woken up as well. Charlotte bent down and gently scratched him behind the ears. Then, she realized: playing with Jelly was what she wanted to do.

She carried Jelly to the couch and patted him all over, hugging him, stroking his fur. They'd never figured out what Jelly was, for he certainly looked like a Black Labrador, but the vets said he was an Australian Shepherd and Border Collie mix. Slowly, she felt sleepy again; and in an instant, she fell asleep with Jelly in her lap.

By the time she woke up, the clock said it was seven-thirty. Mr. Lexington was eating breakfast at the table. Jelly also, somehow, had rolled onto the floor, and he was sleeping with his legs stuck in the air and his tongue sticking out. He was weird that way.

Mr. Lexington looked a little tired, but very attentive. "Oh, hello," he said when Charlotte got up. "Saw you were napping!" He turned back to his breakfast. Charlotte stretched herself. As Mr. Lexington stood up, and as if right on cue, the doorbell exploded.

Ding, ding, ding, ding, ding, ding, ding, ding, ding, ding, ding, dong! Ding, ding, ding, ding, ding, ding, ding, ding, ding, ding, ding, dong! DONG!

"Don't these people know how to use doorbells? You aren't supposed to ring nonstop!" Mr. Lexington complained as he rushed to open the door.

Charlotte tensed. She gasped.

A tall woman stood at the door, presumably Professor Austin. She had long, white, curly hair that fell to her waist. She was covered in black robes, with dark red streaks among the folds. The robes touched the ground, and they dragged behind her as she moved. She had wise-looking blue eyes that scanned the room intently. In her hand, she held a number of scrolls and envelopes.

"Hello, Isaac," she said pleasantly to Mr. Lexington. In shock, Charlotte's uncle stepped aside, and Professor Austin politely invited herself inside.

"It's been a while," she said, looking Mr. Lexington with a smile. "The last I saw you, you were just seven! I remember when Leo, Charlotte's father, was admitted as well, all those years ago…oh yes, what happened to him was a tragedy. He was a very brilliant young student and I enjoyed having him in my classes very much. I'm sorry for your loss."

Mr. Lexington nodded. "Thank you. Please come inside and sit down. So can this magic be inherited?"

"Oftentimes yes, but not always," Professor Austin responded, coming inside. Charlotte looked on, astounded.

Professor Austin paused in the conversation and scanned the tidy home until her eyes rested on Charlotte.

"Just so. Our next young witch! You're Miss Lexington, I take it?" she asked her kindly.

Charlotte nodded nervously.

"Well, well. Let's start!" she said cheerily as she settled herself down on the couch. "Lots to cover today."

"How do you know my uncle?" Charlotte asked.

Professor Austin smiled. "I met him when I first visited your father to tell him he was a wizard. Of course, your uncle was not a wizard, but he was in the vicinity and I made his acquaintance. Now, forty years later, I have come to see you."

"Yes," her uncle chimed in. "I remember when we were kids, and watching football. Leo's favorite team lost, and he did the exact same trick with the television."

Charlotte's mouth fell open. "You knew?" she asked her uncle.

"Yes," he responded. "That's why decided to let you go to Mountain View."

Mr. Lexington smiled and nodded at Charlotte, who gratefully smiled back.

She selected out a roll of bronze parchment as Charlotte took a seat in front of her.

"Now, I'm sure you have browsed Professor Watonburn's letter. It gave you the basic idea. Charlotte, you are a witch, and your blood carries particles known as micromaguses. In fact, all objects, animate or inanimate, carry micromaguses, but only wizards have positively charged micromaguses. A charged micromagus carries a charge that allows you to connect with other objects and send them signals, therefore providing you with the ability to make them do things. In short, a micromagus is a port for thoughts. For example, when you will a mug to fly, the micromaguses in your blood connect with the micromaguses in the mug, telling it to fly."

Professor Austin paused a moment and smiled coyly at Charlotte.

"Of course, as I said, everything contains micromaguses, but only witches and wizards have charged micromaguses. The positively charged ones are the ones that can send out signals; ones that are not charged are used only for receiving signals. That is what makes you special and gives you your ability, Charlotte. Understand?"

Charlotte nodded. "Got it."

"Some objects carry more micromaguses than others, meaning some wizards will be more powerful than others, and some objects may be easier to charm than others, namely the ones with lots of receivers. I am not an expert on this topic, but if you wish to further learn about micromaguses and their effects, I advise you to consider taking bio-magic as an elective."

Charlotte nodded once more, feeling a bit overwhelmed.

"You are a witch with charged micromaguses," summarized Professor Austin, flicking through some scrolls and selecting another one. "Continuing on, the history of Mountain View School is a noble one. We train young wizards and witches to hone their magical ability, and we teach a variety of spells, potions, and other topics. There are several mandatory courses, but we offer a wide selection of electives as well. Here's a list."

Professor Austin *tut-tutted* and handed Charlotte a scroll. Charlotte glanced down for a moment as Professor Austin rifled through her scrolls again.

Instead of regular middle school electives, this list contained not *Home Economics* and *Choir* but things like *Bio-magic* and *Divination*.

"Moving on to regulations. The first and most important rule is that no one is allowed to speak of magic. Everything, Charlotte's ability, Mountain View, and magic in general, must be kept extremely confidential. Though normal people may not realize it, we wizards and witches are, in a way, their guardians. We help keep them safe from harm. The universe is made of two components: Micromaguses and The Fog. The Fog is like an oracle; it writes destinies and stories, and then it executes them. The Fog seeps into minds and puts in thoughts that lead to actions. Some actions and thoughts are benevolent; some are malevolent. The Fog writes many tragedies, though. Us wizards and witches are the only ones who could control its power. It is our mission to protect mankind by warding away the tragedies whenever possible."

"Okay," Charlotte blinked. "Wow, this is a lot to take in."

"I understand, dear," said Professor Austin kindly. "Worry not; you will not have to do anything about the Fog until you graduate three years later."

Charlotte smiled with relief.

"Now, allow me to perform a spell for you!" She pulled out a thin wooden stick from the folds of her robes, what Charlotte deduced was a wand. Professor Austin raised it and waved it—the curtains snapped shut. It was dark. She waved her wand again, and a bright light shot out of her wand tip.

"Yes, dear. It's magic," Professor Austin said as she extinguished her wand and flicked it to reopen the curtains. Warm sunlight flooded back in.

"So, it's like the time I made the coffee mug burning hot, and when

I tipped the hot chocolate!" Charlotte said, astounded.

"Yes. Now..." Professor Austin muttered to herself as she took out another roll of parchment. This one was golden, like the letters Charlotte received from Professor Watonburn.

"That is all of the essentials. Do you have any questions before we move on to getting your school supplies?"

"Er—yes," Mr. Lexington cleared his throat. "As you see, Charlotte is only eight, and I would just like to make sure she is safe. I would like to know exactly where the school is in case of an emergency. It's best if I can tag along and see it for myself, and tour it. You see, all I hope is that this place suits Charlotte well.

Professor Austin considered a moment.

"Normally, non-magic people cannot see or enter Mountain View, but I sympathize with and understand your position. We could make an exception and lift some of the protective magic for one night. I will have to check with the headmaster, but I think he will allow you to accompany us up to the school, and some of the staff would like to give you the tour once you get there. But you cannot delay long, because lifting the protections are dangerous."

"Thank you," replied Mr. Lexington, smiling now. "I got it."

"So, may I introduce you to some guides to take you to Hermes Plaza?" Professor Austin asked.

"Where is that?" Mr. Lexington asked.

"Hermes Plaza. It is a dwelling especially for wizards. It is everywhere and nowhere essentially, but there is an entrance on Pearl Street," Professor Austin replied. "So, yes. May I?"

Professor Austin walked to the door and flung it open with a bang. Mr. Lexington jumped up.

Out there, like they just appeared out of nowhere, was a family of five.

A slim, pretty woman with brown hair curled 40s-style was in front, and a tall sandy-haired man stood right behind the scattered three children. Charlotte went to look them over.

The man and woman wore the same unusual robes as Professor Austin, except the man's was navy blue and the woman's purple.

Charlotte assumed it was the proper wizard wear.

The man stepped into the house. "Hello. You're Mr. Lexington, I take it? I have heard of your research on the wildfires. Thank you for your effort, and I would be quite glad when this whole ordeal has passed. Yes, I am Richard Ross. Call me Richard. Rich too, if you want."

They shook hands.

The woman trotted up the front steps to Charlotte. "Ah, you're Charlotte Lexington, correct? I am Mrs. Ross! This is Sofia, she's graduated from Mountain View already!" she said cheerily as she directed the eldest to her. Sofia was in lilac robes, and she had bright green eyes that neither her father nor her mother shared. She had blonde hair like her mother and a warm smile. Charlotte could tell she was built along the lines of a model student.

"And this is Ace," she beamed, showing her a tall boy clad in a red Letterman jacket. "He's fifteen and starting his last year." He was five foot nine or ten. His hair was sandy like his father's, windswept and parting down the middle. Under his left arm, he carried a football, and he was sturdily built. He gave Charlotte a wink and a smile, his brilliantly white teeth flashing.

"And this is Ella. She's starting Mountain View this year with you!" she turned to a girl half an inch shorter than Charlotte. Ella had blonde hair and bangs. She had sharp beady eyes and a wide smile. Out of all the Ross children, Ella was the plainest. Her sister Sofia was the model student, amiable, smart, probably a Prefect and teacher's pet, gathering from her demeanor. Ace was evidently a star athlete and a good-natured, popular boy. Ella was the most ordinary in the family, not showcasing any specialties, and Charlotte warmed to her because of this.

"Wonderful." Professor Austin gathered her scrolls and envelopes. "I will have to leave now; I have many other students to visit. This afternoon, this family will guide you to Hermes Plaza and assist you with your shopping. Now, now, I must really be off. See you at Mountain View, dears."

She closed the door behind her as she left, leaving the Rosses and Lexingtons staring at each other.

"Uh, shall we leave?" prompted Ella.

"What hosts would we be if we ushered you off in a snap? Sit, let me get some tea for you?" Mr. Lexington said politely.

The Ross family nodded.

Charlotte followed her uncle to the kitchen busied herself, boiling water, counting cups, finding teabags. Smiling to herself, she loaded the china cups all onto a tray to carry them to the living room.

She caught her uncle's weary eye and grinned. "I'll clean these cups by magic," she told him.

"I'm really thinking your powers might be awfully useful," her uncle laughed.

THREE

Hermes Plaza

"I've never been there—Hermes Plaza, I mean," Charlotte said, as she set down the tea tray. "Have some biscuits too."

"Of course you haven't, but I have," Ella replied, smiling as she took a biscuit.

"What's it like?"

"Well, the name is very misleading. It's actually a small Wizarding neighborhood. I even live in there! Towards the back, there are some stores and shops where you can purchase magical items, like wands and potion ingredients. It's the only all-wizard dwelling in all of Midwestern United States, so Mountain View generally recommends students to go there for their purchases."

"Do you use the same money as we do? I'm guessing not," Charlotte continued.

"Well, yes. The ACW—American Confederation of Wizards—decided to switch to dollars a few years ago. It was just so confusing, wizards and witches everywhere having a right fit when it came to going out into the non-magical world," piped up Ace, with another brilliant smile. He tossed his football up in the air and caught it again with one hand.

Ella shook her head and rolled her eyes. "Show-off."

Just then, Mr. Lexington collected himself and walked back into the living room rather awkwardly. They were ready to go shopping for school supplies.

"All right. We'll get everything on your list, Charlotte, then we'll send you back. Tomorrow we can come guide you to school," Mrs. Ross told her.

They put on their shoes and locked the front door behind them.

They took Mr. Lexington's car, a big parade of seven.

As they walked steadily down the street, great furls of smoke curled and billowed out above them, blocking out the sky, blotching it orange and scarlet. A few flakes of ash drifted down from the sky, like snow in midsummer.

"Look at this," Mr. Ross said, as he picked ash out of Ace's hair. "What is the meaning of this? The number of wildfires this year, in the national park and in the towns—ridiculous. I wonder what's causing them. It's not like this year has been particularly dry or hot, it's so strange…"

"Indeed," Mr. Lexington caught on. "How long it has been since I have seen a clear blue sky. And yet, we still have no idea what is causing them."

They got to an ancient bookstore on Pearl Street, which appeared to be closed and out of business. However, that was exactly where Mr. Ross called them together. They huddled against the west wall. "Welcome," he said, "to Hermes Plaza, where you finally cross the magical threshold!" He chuckled and pulled out his wand. He waved it and muttered some words, and then Charlotte was being squeezed through space. It felt like being inside a metal tube. It was pitch-black and very uncomfortable. She felt her stomach being pressed against her, and just as she thought she was going to pass out, they landed in a whole new world.

She struggled to breathe, for the journey almost cracked her ribs.

"Yes, a bit tough the first time. You okay?" Mr. Ross asked Mr. Lexington and Charlotte. Charlotte managed to give a rather feeble nod, but Mr. Ross took it more seriously. He withdrew a dark purple vial from inside his pocket and gave it to Charlotte. "Drink it, it helps," he said. Then, he took out an identical one and handed it to Mr. Lexington.

Mr. Lexington eyed it suspiciously. "Oh no, it's a simple pain-relieving potion. Not poison. I thought it would come in handy since the barrier checks the incomers to make sure they're wizards. It's a bit painful," Mr. Ross told him.

"Yes, but how big of a dosage are we to take?" her uncle asked.

"Er—the entire bottle will suffice."

"Did you measure it?" Mr. Lexington asked worriedly. I am quite afraid to overdose. How many milliliters is it?"

Ella laughed nervously. "Uncle," Charlotte chided. "I think it will be alright to drink the lot."

When Charlotte finished the potion, she felt amazing. A gentle tingling sensation spread throughout her body, warming her up. The ache in her ribs disappeared.

"Feeling better?" Ella asked kindly.

Charlotte smiled wide and meant it. "Yes. Mr. Ross, how does it check for non-magic people, and how'd we get through?" Charlotte asked, always thirsty for knowledge.

"Well, you see, dad waved his wand and said the password. Then, a portal appeared on that bleak wall. It's like a tube, you know. It sucks us all in. Those it recognizes may go through directly, while newcomers have to go through a test to make sure you're magical," Sofia explained.

Charlotte asked again, "But how do the tests work?"

This time, Mr. Ross answered. "It takes you through another tube, this one smaller. So, you feel more pressure. It pushes a sensor into your chest to check the blood your heart is pumping and detects the micromaguses. After this first time, you'll be recorded by the barrier so that next time you don't have to go through the small tunnel."

"So, it basically records data like a computer?" Mr. Lexington asked, trying to sound politely interested.

"Like a what?" Ella asked.

"It's a thing that non-magical people use," Mr. Ross replied. He turned back to Mr. Lexington. "Well, sort of. But it has a mind of its own. It's magic, and it's really complicated, to say the least."

They turned and walked into the plaza. As Ella had described, they first walked into a cozy little village, which looked like a postcard. The houses were very queer, for they were painted bright colors, with oddly designed architecture. The snowcapped Rocky Mountains silhouetted the village, and a wearing cobblestone road wound between the buildings like a many-headed snake. All the inhabitants were carrying wands and dressed eccentrically. Wizards and witches of every age and ethnicity were wandering about their homes. Everyone seemed to know everyone else, and many waved to the Rosses. Charlotte took an immediate liking to this place.

"Hello there, Sofia!" called a middle-aged witch on one side of the cobblestone street, sitting in the shade of her house among the hydrangeas.

"Hi, Ms. Sullivan!" Sofia smiled, crossing over to shake her hand. "How are you?"

"Quite well, quite well," the witch named Ms. Sullivan waved a hand dismissively. "Dear, you have grown quite tall! How is your job?"

"Wonderful," replied Sofia. "The people on the CWE have been very nice to me, and there's never been a shortage of work."

"Good girl," purred Ms. Sullivan, patting Sofia's hand in a motherly fashion. Then, she turned around to gaze at the others in Sofia's party.

"Ace," she noted disapprovingly. "You need to get a haircut. You look like Linda Murphey!"

"Who?" asked Charlotte in an undertone.

"She's some 70s witch," replied Ella. "An actress."

Ace gave Ms. Sullivan a dashing smile in response to her criticism. She didn't take it well. With a huff, she turned to Ella.

"You're so skinny," she said. "Not tall but skinny. Eat up. Also, your bangs are slanted. Who cut your bangs? Not yourself, surely?"

Ella blushed a color of puce as Ms. Sullivan then turned to survey Charlotte.

"Who are you?" she interrogated.

"Charlotte Lexington," responded Charlotte, drawing herself to her full height.

Ms. Sullivan ignored her and turned back to Sofia, who was looking at her siblings and Charlotte apologetically.

"Sofia, dear, go on then. Let me hinder you not, as long as you drop by old Laura Sullivan's some time! It's awfully lonely!"

Sofia nodded and returned to her party with a guilty smile. "It's not my fault I'm the only person in the world she approves of!" she said defensively to Ella, seeing her smirk.

"What's the CWE?" Charlotte asked, exploding with curiosity at everything in this peculiar world.

"The Committee for Wizarding Education," responded Sofia. "I am working for them at the moment."

Soon, the quaint community began fading into a shopping center as they reached downtown. Busy shops lined the streets back and forth, people streaming in and out. "First," Mr. Ross said. "Is Madame Octavia's Bookstore, where you all can get your books."

He led them to what seemed like the busiest shop in the area. It was a simple wooden shack, a hand-painted sign hung outside. In the window displays, stacks of Wizarding Bestsellers, textbooks, and new releases piled to the ceiling.

"Go ahead, take your lists, and find your books. We'll wait outside so it won't be so crowded," Mr. Ross said, giving them each a silvery-colored piece of parchment. Charlotte and Ella looked down at their lists. The lists were written in the same print and in the section about needed books, it said:

Required Books:

1. *Charming Spells: The Entire Collection for Young Wizards* by Catherina Aragona
2. *The Fine Art of Potions* by Skylar Benetton
3. *Transfiguring Objects* by Anastasia Klinski
4. *Magical Plants: Practical and Oriental* by Werner Schmidt
5. *The Book of Defense* by Annie Aldridge
6. *Math for Magical Minds* by Diana-Aida Singh
7. *Language Arts, the Finest Art* by Brenna Katz

They got all the books and walked out to Sofia, Mr. Lexington, Mr. Ross, and Mrs. Ross.

Next, they went to a fabric shop named Candlelight Outfits and got a schoolbag and robes for Ella and Charlotte.

"You look splendid, Ella!" Sofia said after they've fitted her out in the mandatory black uniforms of Mountain View school.

"Black's not really my color," Charlotte said.

"Actually, I think it kind of suits you," Ella shrugged. "I don't know, your brown hair goes nicely with the black."

Next was what Mr. Ross said the most important part: wands.

They went to a little wooden shop called *Vandenberg's Wands*.

"No one really goes here anymore," Mr. Ross said. "It's antique. However, Mr. Vandenberg, the shopkeeper, has studied wandlore for ages. Perhaps he's not as flashy as the modern wand-makers, but his skill is very grounded."

They stepped in. It was dustier than the other shops they had been to. It felt abandoned. But when they stepped in, a rusty bell gave a feeble *ding*, and a man with shoulder-length white hair came out from behind the counter. His face was dirty and wrinkled, and he looked very cranky.

"No one comes to my shop anymore, people! They go to *Dilly Wands*. I think that is the most foolish name ever. Wands contain great power and command great respect! I strive to give them that, while a name like *Dilly Wands* simply dishonors them greatly, you know?" The man said.

"Yes, correct. Do not take it as flattery, my dear man, but you, are the best master of wandlore, Mr. Vandenberg," Mr. Ross kindly replied. "And these two need their first wands. Would you mind?"

Mrs. Ross pushed Charlotte and Ella forward.

"Hello, Mr. Vandenberg, is it?" Ella asked with a big smile on her face.

"Correct, correct." Mr. Vandenberg waved his hand impatiently. "Alright, Miss Lexington first, I need some information."

"Yes?" prompted Charlotte politely as she stepped forward.

"First, the number of letters in your first name?"

"Nine."

"The number of letters in your last name?"

"Also nine."

"Age?"

"Again nine!"

"Gender?"

"Witch."

Mr. Vandenberg screwed up his eyes in concentration. He scribbled on his parchment a moment, then he continued his string of questions.

"Number of family members?"

"Including or excluding myself?"

"Including!" replied Mr. Vandenberg irritably.

"Oh, then two."

"How many siblings?"

"Zero."

"Right- or left-handed?"

"Right."

"How many pets have you had?"

"One."

"Height?"

"Four foot five."

Mr. Vandenberg calculated some more.

"Okay," he finally announced. "Let me take some measurements."

He got out a tape measure and measured Charlotte's right arm, height, wrist diameter, and thumb length. Ella giggled as she watched Charlotte extend her thumb.

Finally, Mr. Vandenberg returned to his quill and parchment. After a moment, he straightened and went to the shelf behind his desk, where thousands of thin wooden sticks were propped up, a label under each of them.

He moved along the shelf, scouring the labels. He picked up wands along the way. He chose six and carried them over to Charlotte. He arranged them on his desktop and presented them to her.

"These six wands have magical properties that suit you," he announced. "The final part is your choice. Choose the wand that will be yours."

"Okay," Charlotte breathed. She picked up the first one, gripped it, and twirled it in her hand. She checked its weight in her hand and pretended to cast a spell with it. She repeated this for the other five wands. Mrs. Ross was jittery with anticipation behind her, and Ella was watching, astounded. Finally, once Charlotte had tried all six wands, she picked up the third and declared, "I like this one."

"This one, eh?" Mr. Vandenberg gave her a coy smile and shoved away the other five wands. He took a look at the wand she had chosen and said, "This is a wand for a smart, strong-willed, and charismatic witch. It is pinewood, the tree from none other than the Rocky Mountains. Ten and a half inches in length, half an inch in base diameter. Are you sure you want this wand?"

"Yes," Charlotte said. Mr. Vandenberg straightened with a smile. He drew out his own wand and tapped Charlotte's.

"Then I pronounce this wand yours."

Mrs. Snow clapped as Charlotte received her wand back from Mr. Vandenberg.

"Congratulations!" cried Sofia, and Ella gave her a hug. Ace clapped her on the back, and Mr. Ross applauded.

Mr. Vandenberg nodded. "Good. Now, come up, Miss Ross, and let's choose your wand."

Ella went through the same questions and measurements. Afterward, Mr. Vandenberg selected five wands for Ella to try. She picked the second in the batch.

Mr. Vandenberg said to Ella, "This is a wand for an empathetic, loyal, and good-natured witch. It is rosewood, imported from India. As you know, rosewood is a beautiful, expensive, and exotic wood with great color and fragrance. Ten inches in length, half an inch in base diameter. Do you want this wand?"

Ella nodded. Mr. Vandenberg tapped her chosen wand with his own and presented it to Ella formally.

"Then I pronounce it yours."

Ella smiled wide and took it from Mr. Vandenberg with a hurried thanks. She then ran into her mother's arms and was cheered by her parents and siblings.

"Congratulations, Miss Lexington, Miss Ross!" Mr. Vandenberg cried, looking cheery for the first time since they entered his shop. "Now come and give your wands a little wave! Let's see their effect!"

Ella went first this time. She raised her wand uncertainly and waved it around her head. Golden mist trailed from her wand-tip, surrounding her, billowing majestically.

"Oh very good, very good!" applauded Mr. Vandenberg, along with Charlotte and the Rosses. "Miss Lexington, let's see yours."

Charlotte withdrew her new wand from within her robes and gave it a complicated twirl. Something misty shot out of it. It was a box, it seemed; inside of it was a sword. The entire Ross family and Mr. Vandenberg gasped. It floated for a while before disappearing.

"What happened?" Charlotte asked.

"It's a long story," Mr. Vandenberg replied darkly, his smile suddenly vanishing. "I'm sure you'll know soon. But, I'm sure, Miss Lexington," he looked at Charlotte closely, "that you will be respected and powerful." He walked away without another word.

They left the money on the counter since he wasn't there to collect it. The experience made Charlotte very uncomfortable.

"Cheer up!" Sofia said once they were outside.

"You know, you are special," Ace added with another wink. Before Sofia could tell him off, for she opened her mouth, he turned and suddenly shouted. "Oh, fantastic! Jude!"

He waved to someone in the crowd. A tall boy with spiky black hair and a mole on his cheek turned. "Ace!" he called.

The two boys bounded towards each other and high-fived. They did a curious little handshake and laughed. Ace turned to go with Jude. "And P.S, for those of you who wanna hear, we'll be at Bounce and Spring!"

"Those two..." Sofia muttered.

"What's this Bounce and Spring?" Charlotte asked, trying to change the subject from herself.

"Oh, Charlotte, it's some sports goods retailer, of course it has to be," Sofia sighed.

When they walked out, Ella spotted someone. "Harry! Harry!" she yelled.

A boy with his mother and father turned. "Harry!" Ella yelled again. "Hi!" Harry replied. "Are you also starting Mountain View?"

"Mhm! And she is too! Charlotte, this is Harry, Harry Snow; Harry, this is Charlotte, Charlotte Lexington. Harry's an old friend of mine."

"Hi," Charlotte said.

"Hello."

Mr. Ross came over. "Hello, Harry. Did you get your pet yet?"

"No, Mr. Ross. But we're on the way now," Harry said.

"Oh, perfect!" Mr. Ross turned to Harry's parents. Mrs. Snow was a tall, slim lady with a thick German accent. She was dressed completely in black, and she had coal liner around her eyes. She had a mole on her left cheek. Her husband was stout in comparison; he had vivid red hair and a French accent.

"Charlotte's parents, or uncle rather, is non-magical. We're going to the bank to exchange some money. Charlotte and Ella are going to check out pets. Would Harry want to go with them?"

"Of course," Mrs. Snow replied. "We're going to go and get some money out of our vault as well. The three little children can go together!"

So, that's how Harry, Ella, and Charlotte went to find a pet while the other Rosses, Harry's parents, and Mr. Lexington went to the bank to exchange and withdraw money.

Bringing a pet of choice was a customary tradition at Mountain View. Students would get to pick any approved animal to bring, though it was not required.

They went to a pet shop named *Eleanor's Pets*. It was busy. The walls were painted bright pink, and perfume drifted through the place. "Honestly," Harry muttered.

"Harry!" Ella said reprovingly. "The scent calms animals."

Ella immediately wandered off to the *Little Critters* section, while Harry went for the *Big Dogs* section. Charlotte didn't know where to go, so she went to the *Birds* section.

In the end, Ella got a ferret she named Peaches, and Harry got a Great Dane named Comet, and Charlotte decided not to get anything since she already had Jelly.

"Just remember not to let Comet too close to Peaches," Ella said. "He might attack her."

"All right, fine!" Harry said.

They found their parents waiting outside, pleased with the pets Harry and Ella had selected.

"But if Charlotte will not get a new pet, then we must get her a present of some sort!" cried Mrs. Ross.

"Nope, I'm okay. Going to Mountain View is probably the best present I've ever gotten!" replied Charlotte, smiling.

"Oh, don't be silly!" Mrs. Ross said, patting her on the back. "Here, what'd you like from Hermes Plaza?"

Charlotte was bustled around by Mrs. Ross until she finally decided that she would like a couple of new books to read. Mrs. Ross looked rather taken aback as Charlotte said this. Charlotte thought that Ace especially would've never asked for books. Mrs. Ross, however surprised, agreed. And so, Charlotte got a heavy bundle of five books.

The books included:

Full History of Mountain View School

Famous Witches and Wizards

Your First Guide to Magic

Magical Encyclopedia Volume 1

Magical Encyclopedia Volume 2

They were so heavy Mr. Ross had to wave his wand to send them back home first.

Both Ella and Charlotte said bye to Harry, and they headed back home.

Back at Charlotte's, they quickly packed everything they needed; Charlotte only took one of her new astoundingly long books, but she took plenty of shorter volumes.

They all returned to Hermes Plaza the next day at eleven o'clock. Whatever their transportation was, it was leaving at midday, sharp. This time though, Charlotte found the way in more comfortable, as promised.

FOUR

Mountain View School of Magic

"It seems we have finally solved the question of what school you will attend!" Mr. Lexington grinned.

Their transportation was a procession of sky-blue carriages pulled by beautiful, snow-white Pegasi. The winged horses stomped the ground and fanned their wings, whinnying impatiently, ready to go. They found a medium-sized carriage due to them being some of the first there, and they poked their heads out of the window when they saw Harry get onto the platform.

"Hey! Join us, Okay?" shouted Ella.

"Charlotte, I've arranged to sit in the head carriage with the caretaker. I'll be up there if you need me, there are a couple of other parents there as well."

"Ok uncle, have a good time!" Charlotte waved at him through the window.

Soon, the caretaker, Mr. Bromhead, hopped out of the lead carriage. He was a wizened old man with a shock of white hair and a walking staff. He had on a dirty brown overcoat, despite the warm weather. He blew a bugle to signal the start of the journey, and they leaned out of the window to wave one last time. Mrs. Ross shouted advice after Ella, and Mr. Ross simply smiled at them all.

The carriages lurched forward, bumping and swaying on the cobblestone. Harry grabbed the edge of his seat nervously.

They were on their way to Mountain View.

The Pegasi did not utilize their magnificent wings however, but merely pulled onwards like regular horses might've done. To Harry's immense relief, the cobblestone road soon wore down into a flat dirt road, which was considerably smoother.

Suddenly, the carriages lurched to a stop, and a girl's shout could be heard.

"What's happening?" Ella asked, poking her head out of the curtains. Charlotte drew her wand even though she could hardly do anything with it yet.

Mr. Bromhead, the caretaker, who was riding in front, jumped off and walked to the girl who was shouting.

"Who are you, and what business do you have here, interrupting our journey?"

"Hello, Mr. Bromhead!" the girl addressed him. "You know me, right? I'm Effir Hosanna, second-year third-tier. I ran a little behind, all because of my newborn brother. But I hope it's not too late to go to school, is it?"

"Do you have any proof that you are a Mountain Viewer? Not an intruder, not a spy?" Mr. Bromhead asked.

Effir laughed. "You know me well! But if you still want proof, here's my letter reminding me of the start of term!"

Mr. Bromhead took a roll of parchment from the girl, Effir, and studied it carefully. He squinted and held it up to the light. He ran a finger over each word and even smelled the parchment. Finally, he rolled it up and nodded to her.

"We have no spare or empty carriages, so is there anyone who would take Miss Effir Hosanna in their carriage?"

"Us!" Ella, always willing to help others, raised her hand.

"Very well, Effir, go ahead!" Mr. Bromhead patted her shoulder.

"Sorry for all the inconvenience, I guess," Effir said as she clambered in. Harry shrugged, and they had a nice talk and played some games together.

"So, where is Mountain View?" inquired Charlotte after a while.

"On the side of Longs Peak," answered Ella immediately. "It's well-protected against the hikers; it's far from the trails. But when the occasional poor folk comes wandering around, it usually results in an accident. All of those mountaineering accidents on Longs Peak… they're usually due to the anti-non-magic protections."

"Longs Peak is known as deadly for this reason," Harry shook his head. "Unfortunate."

Charlotte opened the window and peered out. They were already leaving town. The mountains loomed majestically over them, closer than ever. The dwellings and buildings were thinning out to the countryside.

Charlotte went to read a book, and after two hours or so, the procession stopped again.

They were at a small service center on the side of a deserted stretch of road.

"Snack stop!" Mr. Bromhead hollered just as someone knocked on the door and asked, "Anything sweet? Anything you want to eat? Anything you want to drink?"

"Oh, food!" Ella said excitedly as she slid the door open. She took out her money purse and went to buy mountains of snacks.

"No need to thank me for these sweets," Ella said as she sat down and passed them around.

Effir didn't want candy, so she just ate some sandwiches she had made and brought with her. "They're rather nice," Effir explained. "I made them myself, peanut butter and strawberry rhubarb jam, my favorite."

Charlotte found the candy Ella bought very unusual because she was accustomed to snacks like fruit gummies and animal crackers, but instead there were "Rude Chips," for they made weird noises as they were munched on; there were "Exploding Bonbons," which exploded as soon as they touched your tongue, splattering the inside of your mouth with chocolate; and "Ever-Lasting Fruit Rolls," which were typical fruit rolls, but they didn't end until you told them to!

They talked, played games, read books, and ate more snacks on the way. Meanwhile, acres and acres of green country farmland passed by outside. Rows of wheat, corn, and alfalfa as well as herds of cattle and horses rolled past as the sun started dipping. Slowly, the mountains engulfed them, forming a semi-circle around them. The flat terrain crossed into mountainous, hilly terrain. They were now sharply inclined, the carriages proceeding in a single file through a clearing of aspen and pine trees. But the view was not very enjoyable, for the smoke had become thicker as they advanced.

"It is so strange," Harry picked up on the conversation Charlotte had had all too frequently these days. "It's not just this year; the number of wildfires in the last five years have been increasing too."

Before Ella could respond, the carriages stopped, and Mr. Bromhead jumped off the head carriage and called, "It's about time to change into your new robes, we're almost there!"

They had arrived at a small public bathroom, and the students lined up. Charlotte groaned, knowing she'd have to wait forever, as there were many students, but it was a small facility. To her amazement, thirty cubicles fit inside the place.

They soon changed from their jeans and t-shirts to the school robes they picked up from Hermes Plaza and hopped back onto their carriage, giddy with excitement.

Not long after they continued, Mr. Bromhead shouted once more.

"Please gather your bags and your pets, and please do not forget any possessions! Everything found left aboard will be tossed! We have now reached the final phase of our journey. The road is too steep, so we fly—!"

Suddenly, the door slammed open. Ace stood there and beamed.

"Just welcoming you to Mountain View!" he explained good-naturedly. His sandy hair was windswept, and he still carried the football under one arm. Charlotte distinctly saw three girls peeking out of another carriage, eyeing him hopefully. Ella snorted.

"Wait, how'd you get here?" Charlotte asked, amazed, as he steadied himself on the threshold.

"A little magic, of course!"

"Remember Brown?" Ace then asked Ella. "The one with the

pointed nose and those water-blue eyes, yes. She's here! Oh, couldn't she have been, like, a little younger?"

Ella frowned at the news.

"Enemy," she explained to Charlotte and Harry, but the horses were already breaking into a trot, picking up speed, like a plane taxiing before take off.

"Gotta go!" Ace said, and he shrunk into a hawk and sailed into another carriage. Charlotte pulled the door closed behind them just as the Pegasi started galloping.

"Hold on!" Ella advised, clenching the carriage door, her face white. In one glorious moment, the sound of graveling crunching under the wheels subsided, and they climbed steeply into the air. Harry was thrown into the others as the Pegasi ascended at a dangerously sharp angle.

Once they had reached sufficient altitude, however, the angle flattened and the flight became gradually smoother. Once everyone had gotten used to the sensation of flying, they all relaxed and began excitedly looking out the window.

But all too soon, they were descending. Charlotte looked out of the window. Through the smoke, she could see they were headed for the side of Longs Peak.

With a sickening thump, the carriage touched down, along with the Pegasi. The Pegasi taxied a moment before finally coming to a halt.

They streamed out with the rest of the students, and right in front of them was the giant school. They had arrived at Mountain View School of Magic.

But the strange thing was, Charlotte couldn't seem to make out the building's definite shape. It flickered and changed like a mirage: one minute, it was a cabin, just like what you'd see on a beach, but it changed, morphing into something vaguely like the Senate House.

After a few seconds of indecision, a voice spoke in her mind: *"Magic detected, precautions no longer necessary."*

Suddenly, all images of a cabin went *poof*, and in front of Charlotte was a tall, handsome, Romanesque castle complete with five towers, the North, South, East, West, and Center ones. It was nestled into the side of the mountain, surrounded by old, tall coniferous trees.

In front of the castle was a sparkling navy-blue lake. A small stream wound down like a ribbon from the top of the mountain and trickled into the lake reservoir. There was a calming sound of flowing water as the stream emptied into the lake.

It was intricately decorated. From afar, all Charlotte could make out were blinding white lights flickering around it, which, according to what she'd read, was the signal for the First Day feast.

It was a cloudless night, cool and beautiful, like summer nights are. A waning moon hung above the castle's highest turret, and the breeze made little ripples on the lake surface. Fireflies buzzed around their heads, and even the air was fresh on this sheltered side of Longs Peak.

"I can't believe this is real!" Charlotte gasped as she walked up to the grand staircase with Ella and Harry. "Wow!"

Charlotte walked slowly, entranced, past the beautiful grounds, gradually approaching the enormous looming castle.

Now that she was closer, Charlotte could see the famous carvings of magic: people waving wands, sitting over potion cauldrons, confronting black clouds, which Charlotte knew was the Fog.

The magical part was that all these carvings moved, and around each frame were four pearls studded into the wall. Charlotte wondered avidly about the net worth of this school.

Inside was warmly lit with torches giving off a faint golden light. The entrance hall had a big archway, looking very grand, making everything feel like a dream.

Then, Professor Austin strode out from behind big doors and addressed the students.

"Second and third years, head into the hall and take your positions at the correct table. First-years, wait here." She opened the door a crack, and the other students filed in.

She turned to the first-years. "Leave your bags here; we will bring them to your dorms."

She opened the door to check on the students before peeking back out and saying, "Come in."

She opened the doors nice and wide to reveal a big dining hall bathed in the same golden torchlight. She led them in.

"First-years, to the table on the very left."

Five long tables were placed in the hall. Four were vertical, and one was at the front of the room, placed horizontally. The Head Table was filled with professors. Beneath were three tables. The one on the very left, where first-years sat, was completely empty.

A round of cheers and loud clapping filled the hall as the first-years walked past.

When everyone quieted down, Professor Austin cleared her throat and unrolled a piece of parchment.

"Students, welcome or welcome back to Mountain View School of Magic! Our honorable school has educated wizards and witches for over twenty-four generations to take up wizardkind's noble quest to protect against the Fog.

"Our beautiful school is concealed in the Rocky Mountains, on the side of Longs Peak. Here, our excellent professors teach our students a number of important wizarding topics to aid them in their careers.

"At Mountain View, the student body is sorted into three groups: Top-tier, second-tier, and third-tier. Students are sorted in their first year depending on academic excellence, and their curriculums will be adjusted in accordance with their scores.

"Tomorrow morning, first-years will attend an entrance exam and afterward select electives. Older students who wish to retake the test to replace in a different group must come see me in my office this evening before ten. Classes officially begin on Monday, August 26th, the day after tomorrow.

"Before our feast, each group is invited to sing their group song!"

She pointed to the table where the students in the second-tier group were sitting, and they began.

"We are the second-tier of Mountain View,
We don't have extra talents.
But we are always on level—
Never too high or too low!
We are the Second-tiers,

And we are so proud!
We will remain faithful to ourselves—
All throughout!

They finished their song, and the hall erupted into polite applause. Professor Austin then pointed at the Top-tier Group.

We are the Top-tier in our school,
always excelling!
They say we are too smart,
We are too good,
But we remain humble.
We love who we are,
And so let it be,
Let no more changes happen!

Everyone clapped once more. Professor Austin smiled and clapped serenely along. As the noise died away, she directed the third-tier Group to sing.

We, the third-tier in Mountain View,
we are—
But we aren't discouraged,
We are still us,
And it doesn't matter what others think.
We are happy with who we are,
Who we are!

There was more clapping for this song than any of the others in order to encourage them.

Professor Austin raised her hands, and everyone quieted.

"Let the feast begin!"

The doors to the hall were flung wide open, and in tromped twenty people, dressed in white. Charlotte recognized them as waiters. They each pushed a cart laden with delicious-smelling food.

They walked around the tables, carefully placing dishes on the tables in between students. Once everything had been settled, they wheeled now empty carts out of the hall in a single file, and the doors closed behind them.

At once, the noise level in the hall took a sharp upswing. The teachers on the Head Table started eating, and so Charlotte and Ella laughed and dug into their plates of roast chicken.

The meal was delicious. It tasted home-cooked, and it was warm and fresh. There were dozens of different dishes, different kinds of soup, different kinds of bread, many varieties of meat, and lots of foreign dishes as well. There were drinks of all kinds and even a luxurious selection of dessert.

When the feast ended, and everyone was stuffed, the food just disappeared, their plates were wiped clean and spotless. A moment later, they disappeared completely.

Professor Austin began talking. "Everyone, please listen to Headmaster Professor Watonburn, for he has important news!" Professor Watonburn, an old man with trimmed, greying hair, stood up. Despite his age, he looked powerful and energetic.

"Thank you, Athena. I remind you all that no one is permitted to leave the school grounds except on the weekends. On Saturday, the gates are open for students to explore the surrounding mountains. The entire Rocky Mountain range is open, but all students must return by nightfall. Mingling with non-magical people or going down into dwellings is prohibited.

"Well, Professor Austin has already summarized the important points. Return to your dorms. Rest well!"

FIVE

The Entrance Exams

Professor Austin came over to usher the first-years to a temporary dorm on the second floor of the school. Ella, Harry, and Charlotte were deep in discussion about the Dungeon when they realized their fellow first-years had left. Charlotte put a hand on Ella's shoulder. "Come on, got to go up to sleep! Mountain View does have a curfew like every other boarding school, Ella!"

She directed them towards the crowd of first-year students that were following Professor Austin. Taking one last look at the Dining Hall, she twisted around, her robe sweeping the floor, and hurried after the now almost long gone first-year students.

In the entrance hall, Charlotte spotted her uncle talking with Professor Austin. She deviated toward him.

"Hi uncle!"

"Hello Charlotte," Mr. Lexington responded. "Well, I've taken the tour and I know the place. I think you will like it here. After all, if they teach magic, you've got lots of new and exciting topics to learn. I like the environment too. I'm off now, but write to me at least once a week and inform me if anything happens, alright?"

"Ok uncle, goodbye, take care and good luck on your research!" Charlotte said, giving him a hug.

Mr. Lexington soon departed, and Professor Austin bade them hurry up to their dormitories. As they climbed to the top of the stairs—

"What is this?" a brisk voice snapped behind them. The three of them jumped. "What are you doing, out of bed at this hour? Go immediately to your dooms, you little twits!"

"Yes, Professor," Ella replied. "But, it's our friend, she sort of—"

"Silence!" growled the teacher. "Nobody cares. Go now!"

This teacher spoke extremely rapidly, his words shot out like a machine gun.

Charlotte, Ella, and Harry nodded and they headed up the tower. They could feel the teacher's eyes on their backs.

"Jeez," Charlotte couldn't help whispering to Harry.

The next morning, they woke up early. Last night, Professor Austin had assigned bunks to all the first-years in one large dorm, and she told them the caretaker, Mr. Bromhead, would wake them on time.

At seven in the morning, Charlotte heard a brass bell ringing away in the distance. She opened her eyes, for all night, she'd been afraid to be late.

The other first-years were rising around her. Mr. Bromhead strode between the four-poster beads, striking a bell and ringing it in sleeping people's faces.

Charlotte yawned. She looked around and saw Ella staring back at her.

"Morning," they called to each other.

After they had changed into robes, they were led back down to the dining hall by Mr. Bromhead, where they once again took their seats at the fourth table.

"What do you think they'll test us on?" Charlotte asked nervously. "I've never studied any magic in my life."

"Oh, Charlotte," Ella laughed. "You'll do wonderful. According to Sofia, they'll test our micromagus number, make us take aptitude tests, and we have to take some basic non-magical courses too, like math and English. Then they give us this sheet where you have to write down your special abilities, such as being multilingual or being really good at sports."

"So no magical tests?"

"Well, the micromaguses count as that."

"Oh yeah, I see."

"Hey, where's Harry?"

Harry joined them later. In front of the whole school, he was shoved into the dining hall by Mr. Bromhead. He was shouting something about Harry being "a lazy, good-for-nothing sleeper."

After breakfast, Professor Austin, now in robes of magenta, with her white hair flowing behind her as usual, came to take the first-years to an exam room.

This room was nearly as big as the dining hall, with a high domed ceiling that was made mostly of glass, so that it let in a lot of natural light. About one hundred or so desks were placed around the hall. Niches lined the walls, in which marble busts stood, gleaming under the bright sunlight.

Professor Austin read names off a scroll and directed students to sit at their assigned desks. Once everyone was settled in alphabetical order by last name, Professor Austin opened the door again and led in nine other witches and wizards. Some of them Charlotte recognized from the Head Table, so she assumed they must also be teachers.

"Students," Professor Austin announced. "Welcome to the Mountain View School Entrance Examinations. Today, you will be put through five separate exams to determine the group into which you will be sorted. Let me remind you that the top-tier students are the most academically excellent, second-tier takes the average, and third-tier takes the bottom scorers.

"The first examination will take place in five minutes. My fellow professors here and I will take measures of your micromagus density.

"The second and third examinations are for your basic subjects: mathematics and language arts, rudimentary skills needed all throughout your life.

"The fourth examination is an aptitude test. Similar to what many non-magical people refer to as an IQ test, this examination tests your problem-solving and critical thinking skills.

"Last but not least is the extra credentials examination. If you believe there is anything that sets you apart or makes you special, you may write it down on a sheet to be handed in at the end of the exam. If you are multilingual, are a descendent of a famous witch or wizard, have earned any academic awards in your education in the non-magical society, feel free to write it down. If you have any impressive achievements, any special skill sets, feel free to record them. Think of this as your résumé.

"So, young witches and wizards of tomorrow, let the examinations begin!"

Charlotte took a deep breath. She was in the fourth row. The ten professors each selected a column and began pressing a sensor-like object to the first student's wrist, seemingly scanning the bloodstream. After they finished, they scribbled a number onto a sheet and moved on.

When it was Charlotte's turn, she presented her wrist to a stout, balding old wizard.

"Lexington, Charlotte!" he paused knowingly before smiling at her. "May I please see your wrist, now?"

He pressed the sensor to Charlotte's outstretched wrist. It was pure silver and freezing cold to the touch. It beeped thrice. He peered at the little number that showed up on the screen.

"Oh my!" he squinted at the numbers. "An extraordinary amount indeed. Ah, this reminds me of Barnaby Faulkner, I taught him. Do you know the legend of the Great Barnaby Faulkner? You have as many micromaguses as him dear! A powerful witch you will be! This is a very good score!" He laughed and recorded the number, which he kept from Charlotte's view. He moved on. Charlotte exhaled. There was one exam she hadn't failed.

She breezed through mathematics. It being one of her best subjects, she calculated the sums, did long division, did the multiplication, solved the algebraic equations, measured the angles for geometry, and used those formulas for the volumes of different prisms she memorized.

Language Arts was a tad bit more difficult, but easy by comparison nonetheless. While people scratched their heads around her, she read through the long texts and understood the vocabulary words. Perhaps that'll be two more examinations she hadn't failed?

The hardest one was the aptitude tests. Charlotte was smart, but her weak point was finding patterns. She peered at the different colored shapes, the numbers arranged in the wrong orders, and tried to make sense of them. However, she still thought she did very well still.

Finally, Professor Austin handed her an Extra Credentials sheet. She looked down and ticked multilingual, adding as a note she had taken German and Spanish for a long time.

She ticked Academic Awards, listing down the many competitions she won, and the awards received.

She ticked Artistic Talents, for she played the violin.

Finally, when she handed in all five examinations, she exhaled. That was that. She couldn't have done too bad. If the aptitude grades didn't drag her down, she should make it into top-tier. She met Ella and Harry outside of the exam room.

"Oh it was horrible!" Harry complained. "The math exam, I'm sure I failed."

"It was alright," Charlotte said.

"I'm sure you'll make up for your math grade with your Extra Credentials grade. You play all those sports! If you guys should be worried for anyone, it's me."

"Nonsense," Charlotte retorted. "You'll have aced the aptitude exam."

"That's one out of five, Charlotte."

They stood in the hall, discussing their scores and checking answers with each other. Finally, when all the other students had left, Professor Austin emerged with two other teachers. They were each carrying a stack of exam papers.

"Well, Lennox, Diane, we'll need those graded by lunch so I can pass them out to the students," Professor Austin was saying.

"Certainly, certainly!" the witch named Diane responded airily. "I'll send them to your office when I'm done?"

"Please do," Professor Austin responded. She and the two other teachers proceeded down the hall, not having noticed them huddled behind the door. "Oh, and please remember what I said, about the girl,

Charlotte. I'm not sure if Miss Lexington will choose your electives, but if she does, you have to foster her well. She is chosen for a great destiny, and very bright herself. She is truly something special. Protect her."

With that, the teachers turned a corner and disappeared from view.

Charlotte, Ella, and Harry turned to look at each other.

"What was that about?" Charlotte asked, intrigued.

"Do you think... that symbol that appeared from your wand... at Vandenberg's?" Ella suggested.

"Maybe, yeah that would make sense!" Charlotte said.

"What symbol?" Harry asked, as they started down the hall after Professor Austin.

They explained the events of that day to Harry, and then they started discussing the meaning of Professor Austin's words. When they went back to their dormitory, Mr. Bromhead was handing out electives sheets. He emphasized that they should merely look through subjects they were interested in, but some of the electives only took certain tiers, so they shouldn't be so sure yet.

After lunch, the grades returned. Professor Austin handed out sheets with the statistics of each student's scores, the areas they need to improve upon, and their sorted group.

Fingers crossed, Charlotte thanked Professor Austin and looked down at her sheet.

Her micromagus exam was her highest score, mathematics closely following, then the extra credentials, then language arts, finally her aptitude exam was her weakest point. All of them were in the top 10 percentile however, her micromagus was in the top 1 percentile, and her math was top 3.

Finally, she closed her eyes and reopened them. She took a deep breath and looked further down the page.

SORTED GROUP: Top-tier

She gasped with excitement and looked at Ella and Harry on her right. "I'm top-tier!" she exclaimed. Harry was, too.

Ella stayed silent. Charlotte peered over her shoulder: second-tier.

"Aw, Ella," Charlotte put an arm around her. "It's alright. You did well still!"

Ella shrugged and laughed nervously. "Yeah, I guess."

"Cheer up, little sis!" Ace appeared behind her, flanked by Jude and a tall Black boy. "You don't wanna be a nerd. Second-tiers are cool!"

Ella laughed and aimed a kick at his shin. Ace sat down beside them. He tossed his football up in the air and then caught it again with amazing agility.

"Ah, the Rosses," a drawling voice sounded behind them. Suddenly Ella's face fell, and she clenched her fists. Her knuckles became pearly white.

"Go away, Penelope." Ella didn't even turn around as she spoke.

"Aw, Ella," Penelope was another first-year girl. She had the bluest eyes Charlotte had ever seen, and they sparkled when she looked at people. Her hair was the lightest blonde, not a streak of anything darker. They were arranged into two long braids down her shoulders. She was flanked by two boys, sturdily built, a little pudgy, and menacing-looking, though Charlotte thought they also looked rather dim-witted. Penelope sat down beside Ella. "What's wrong? Got sorted into second-tier? Oh, don't worry. You and your whole family are doomed to always be second class, always be overshadowed. Accept it, don't take it personally. You wanna know why? I don't know, it's just your fate."

"Ignore her," Ace said coolly.

"Mind your manners," Penelope said, relaxed. "You should respect me, commoners."

"Who's so high and mighty now?" Ella snapped. "Besides, Sofia was top-tier, my father was top-tier too!"

Penelope shrugged. "Luck."

Ella looked at the two boys behind Penelope. "What are Sam and Bob? Bottom tier? Oh, Penelope, if you want to be so great, you're gonna need better company."

"Sam and Bob are second-tier," growled Penelope.

"Your majesty, I'm afraid you didn't hear. Leave!" Jude piped up.

Penelope took her time, smiling fake-innocently out of her crystal-clear blue eyes. She slowly stood up, carefully arranged one of her blonde braids, and walked off, holding her chin up, not at all intimidated.

"Penelope Brown," muttered Ella. "Like she's a princess. She and her whole family are criminals. You don't know their history."

"Come on now, electives!" Charlotte said, pulling out her sheet, trying to distract Ella. "What do you want to take? I'm very interested in bio-magic," Charlotte said.

"Bio-mag?" Harry asked. "Yeah, my mom took that when she was here. She said it's a waste of time."

"How come?"

"The professors hardly know anything, the whole course is just like, 'this is *probably* how the micromagus works, but *we really don't know anything*.'"

Charlotte laughed. "Biology isn't just about the micromaguses right? There are plants and stuff."

"Yeah but they dedicate two out of the three years you take this course just to micromaguses, so either way you'll still spend most of your time in that course listening to uncertainties."

"I'm taking History of Magic," decided Ella. "I wanna know all about the tyrannies and dark wizards."

"What elective do you think will enable us to learn about the Dungeon of Unknown Doom?" asked Charlotte.

"Advanced Spells and Curses," Harry pointed out.

"History of Magic," said Ella again.

"I'll take both?" shrugged Charlotte. "And one more…"

"What do you like? The outdoors? Science?"

"Science," agreed Charlotte. "STEM."

"What stem? Like the stem of a flower? You want bio-mag?"

"No, it stands for Science, Technology, Engineering, and Mathematics," laughed Charlotte. "I guess wizards don't have that?"

"Nope," said Ella. "But what field of science? Biology or physics or chemistry?"

"Astrophysics,"

"Take Astro-mag!"

"Do you just put 'mag' at the end of everything?"

"Hey, now that I think about it, yes!"

They laughed. Ella seemed to forget about her predicament and laughed with them.

SIX

Friends and Foes

But after dinner, Professor Austin separated the first-years into three groups. Harry and Charlotte reluctantly bade Ella goodbye, assuring her that they would still hang out together after lessons.

Ella nodded, not looking at them, abashed.

Charlotte, Harry, and the other top-tier first-years followed Mr. Bromhead to their dormitory.

At the same time, Professor Austin led the second-tiers to their dorm. As Ella shuffled along, her eyes on her shoes, a girl approached her.

"Hey," the girl said. "I'm Selena."

Ella looked up. She had dark eyes and long, wavy, sleek dark hair. She was an inch taller than Ella.

"Hey," Ella replied half-heartedly. "Ella."

"Nice to meet you then, Ella," Selena smiled. "Something wrong? You don't look very happy."

"Yeah, well you're right," Ella sighed. "I'm not."

"Wanna tell me?"

Ella raised an eyebrow suspiciously. Selena raised both hands in surrender.

"I'm just trying to be your friend," Selena explained. "But if you don't want to talk..."

"No, I'm sorry," Ella said, quickly grabbing her wrist. "Don't go, I want to talk."

Selena smiled and nodded. Ella launched into a long explanation about her friendship with Harry and Charlotte, the way her examinations went, what happened between them, and everything else in between. Selena listened patiently at her side.

"Well, I'm just kind of sad to be separated from them," Ella complained to Selena as they ascended the stairs. "I've known Harry since we were three, and Charlotte was my new best friend here. I'm not jealous, I just want to help. This is a lot of pressure to be going through alone, right?"

"Well, yes," Selena said. "Definitely. But she's got Harry, after all."

"Yeah, for sure," Ella said. "But I want to be there for her."

"Ella," Selena laughed. "It's not like you're never going to see them again!"

Ella laughed too. "What was I thinking?"

Her eyes fell on Sam and Bob, who were slouching behind Professor Austin.

"You know that girl Penelope? She's a bully," she nodded at Sam and Bob.

"Oh yeah," Selena whispered back. "I saw them push two other first-years out of their seats today."

"Not surprised."

Selena shrugged. She paused a moment, then, "Hey, Oliver!" she yelled at a boy in the hallway, also second-tier, walking with them to the dorms.

He turned around. "Oh, Selena. I didn't know you were here too. Isn't it amazing? Suddenly being wizards and learning magic and everything?" he asked.

Oliver was a bespectacled Asian boy with brown hair and almond eyes. He gave Ella a smile.

"Hello," he said. "I'm Oliver. I'm biracial, my mom was Japanese but my dad's American."

"Hi," replied Ella with a smile.

"Yup! I think it's just weird sometimes to be non-magical," Selena shrugged. "My parents, though, were both educated at Mountain View. Oh yes, a witch and a wizard!" She proudly ended.

"Nice," Ella nodded. "But we're way behind everyone else. We gotta go!" And they ran up the steps and towards their dorm. They got up the twisting staircase as the last student was filing in, and the door just vanished, popped out of existence.

"How're we supposed to get in?" Ella asked.

"I have no idea," said Selena. "I think the Prefects were supposed to tell us. I saw them at the front of the line. I hope to be one once I reach my third year!"

"But we missed them," Oliver said. "Uh oh!"

Just then, the very same teacher who confronted Harry, Ella, and Charlotte last night walked up to them, already using magic to write out detention slips.

"Ross, is it? Being out of bed when you're not supposed to has become a recurring habit for you. Maybe if we deprived you of sleep for a week you would learn to respect the curfew."

Selena replied. "Please, sir. We r-r-ran a little b-behind them, and we d-d-didn't hear the p-p-p-prefect tell us how to get in!"

As the teacher opened her mouth to ask something else, the door suddenly appeared, and a boy and girl were standing there.

"Oh no, we're three students short, Kat!" the boy said. Then he saw the teacher, Ella, Selena, and Oliver standing there.

"Oh, hello, Professor Tantalus! Excuse me, but I believe those are the missing students, can we please have them?" he asked.

Professor Tantalus , as he was called, whirled around. He frowned. "Only this time, your insufferable child. Can you not even manage twenty eight-year-olds? I shall have a word with the headmaster about your abysmal performance as Prefect." And he headed down the steps.

"We're so sorry, we just—" Selena tried to say to the Prefects.

"No, it's fine," the boy Prefect said. Then, he leaned in and softly whispered, "Watch out for Professor Tantalus, he's really, like the terror of the school. On another note, hello, I'm Herald, this year's Second-tier Prefect." He gestured to the girl beside him. "And this is Katherine, the other Prefect."

He turned back to the girl. "Kat, let's show them how to get in."

Katherine nodded and reached for her wand. "You tap this brick—"

she said, prodding with her wand at the only grey brick on the wall of red "—and say the password. Remember, the password changes each Sunday, so before you leave the room, ask a Prefect about it. Right now, it's 'Fluffy Unicorns'!"

Katherine smiled, so did Ella and Selena. However, Oliver and Herald looked revolted.

Suddenly, the brick popped out of place and showed a small hole.

"Um, there's no way I'm ever going to fit in there!" Selena said as Katherine and Herald laughed.

"There will be one more password that will never change," Herald explained. "And that is…"

"Your name, your group, your school," said `Kat. Oliver frowned.

"Your entire name, the group you're in, which is Second-tier, and your school, Mountain View School of Magic. Let me show you."

She positioned herself right in front of the hole the brick had left and said, "Katherine Alexandra Howard, Second-tier Group, Mountain View School of Magic!" Immediately, the hole became bigger and revealed a tapestry stitched with a big S for 'second-tier' hanging to block their sight of the room. Kat simply shoved the tapestry out of the way and stepped in, and the hole became smaller, the brick popped back into place, and it was as motionless as ever.

"Why don't you try?" Herald asked Ella. Ella nodded, and as she drew out her wand, she heard a faint step that echoed down the winding stairwell. She whirled around. There was no one there.

"What was that?" Charlotte asked as well. They shrugged. Convinced that it was the wind, Ella prodded the brick.

"Fluffy unicorns!"

The brick popped out, and she continued, "Ella Elena Ross, Second-tier Group, Mountain View School of Magic!" She shoved aside the tapestry and looked around the room. It was warm and spacious, and the wallpaper was blue with purple stars. A roaring fire stood at the far end of the room, and a rich navy carpet was stationed in front of it. On the carpet were two big cushioned armchairs, draped with a luxurious gold blanket on the backrest. Between them sat a wooden table with a vase full of forget-me-nots. Smaller armchairs and tables were positioned around the room, as well as beanbags of all shapes and sizes. The pleasant fragrance of burning wood filled the common room.

Behind her, Selena came in, also gaping at the place. Then came Oliver, followed by Herald. "Pretty neat, right?" Herald said. "You see those staircases?" he asked, pointing at two sets of stairs on the far side of the Common Room. "The right one leads to the girls' dorms, and the left leads to the boys' dorms."

Oliver bid them goodbye and followed Herald.

Ella and Selena walked up the other set of stairs.

At the top of the stairs, Kat was waiting for them in front of three doors. "Good, I see you've learned how to get in. She showed them the first door. "First-years in here."

She gave them one last smile and closed the door behind them.

Inside were the only other two Second-tier first-year girls, Amy Chase and Jenna Johnson. They each had a four-poster bed with a blue bedspread, pillows, and blanket. They each had a bulletin board behind their bed and a small closet.

Amy was sticking a family photo on her board, and Chloe was hanging a banner with the words, **Another Witch!**

Ella smiled when she saw her trunk and backpack had already been placed at her bedside. She opened it to take out a poster of some wizarding musical and pinned it on her board along with her class schedule.

Selena took out her schedule too, but she pinned Mountain View's coat of arms on her board.

"Hi guys," Ella said.

"Hi!" said Jenna.

"Hello," Selena said pleasantly.

"What classes do we have tomorrow?" Ella asked, changing the subject.

"Depends on your electives!"

"Ah, right."

"Well, I'm tired," Amy said, and stuffed her schedule along with her books in her backpack. "Good night!"

They all tucked themselves in and followed her example.

Ella sighed contentedly and shut her eyes. The gentle tinkling sound of water dripping into the reservoir lake sounded like wind chimes...

Little did she know tomorrow was going to be a lot more than she expected.

The next morning, they headed back down to the Dining Hall for breakfast.

After, their first class was charms. Selena, Ella, and Oliver entered the classroom nervously and found seats. Once the bell rang and the room was full, Professor Sparks, their teacher, drew the curtains half-closed so that they were plunged into a mysterious semi-darkness.

"Students!" he called cheerily, yet also mystically. "Welcome to Mountain View! Dear Professor Austin has informed me that today I have the honor of being the first-year second-tiers' first class! Now, the first formal magical class of your life is always an important rite-of-passage. Yes, we will be proceeding to some basic spell-casting today, but firstly, many things need to be explained."

He paused a moment and beamed at them all. Then, he waved his wand, and strands of shiny gold wound out of it. Selena gasped. The strands wound themselves into the shape of a person.

"To those who have been born to magical families, and already know about micromaguses and basic spell-casting, I still beg for your attention, as there are many important topics I will be covering today that you may not have had a completely thorough knowledge of before. Also, you might want to take notes."

With a little wink at the class, he flicked his wand, and the strands began moving again. At the same time, he began narrating.

"A wizard's power comes from the micromaguses in his bloodstream—" At this, the strands gave the effect of zooming in upon the person's arm. Small golden particles were moving inside, representing micromaguses. "A wizard has charged micromaguses, while non-magic people and inanimate objects have micromaguses that are not charged. Charged micromaguses can send out signals at the wizard's will; the un-charged micromaguses can only receive the signals.

"When a signal is received, it will cause the object to do what the wizard in particular willed it to do. For example, if I cast a spell on a book, telling it to move, the charged micromaguses in my blood will send out a signal to the micromaguses in the book. The book will heed my instructions and move."

The golden strands wound themselves into a book. The book shifted to the right at these words.

"Micromagus signals do not only tell existing objects to do things, in fact, they can conjure up objects from thin air, by manipulating the micromaguses in the air. But that is more advanced. You will not learn such magic until your third-year, it is not necessary to discuss at the moment. Is everyone following me?"

Ella, Oliver, and Selena nodded along with the rest of the class.

"Very good!" said Professor Sparks jovially. "Now you know how spells are put into effect, I'm sure you're all very curious to learn of the way spells are made.

"Spells are simpler than imagined; you merely point your wand directly at the object—there are specifics to help you achieve better results, which you will learn in due course—and will it to do what you wish. We begin with verbal incantations, then we proceed to doing it silently. Spells are sorted into four categories.

"The elementary level consists of spells that move or change the appearance of an object. For example, if I were to change the color of this piece of paper, or make it throw itself into the trash bin, that would be elementary level magic.

"The secondary level changes an object's elemental properties. Do not think of magic as being merely miraculous; it is based on science! If I were to change the genetic makeup of a student or to transform one element into another—such as H_2O into CO_2—that would be secondary level.

"Once you reach the intermediate level, you shall begin to learn to conjure and create objects out of thin air. This is the moment when you can shape something out of nothing.

"Lastly, the expert level. The most difficult, magic on this level requires strong emotional and mental will. The expert level often meddles in the change or control of personalities, wills, emotions, and minds. Only the bravest of heart, cleverest of skill, and strongest of will can successfully perform expert level magic."

Professor Sparks paused. The class looked expectantly at him.

"Well, aren't you copying this down?" he asked.

Ella hurriedly lowered her eyes to her notebook, writing down each level of magic and its uses. Once the scratching of pens on paper had subsided, Professor Sparks began again.

"In your first year, you will be confined to level 1 magic. In your second year, you shall explore level 2, as well as parts of level 3. In the final year, you will carry on with level 3, and then, only select students will be taught level 4. Level 4 magic is dangerous when used incorrectly, and terrible when used with ill intentions... well, I am getting ahead of myself. You need not know this until your final year...

"Well, that would be it," said Professor Sparks, looking through a sheaf of parchment on his desk. "Now, one last thing. I'm sure you all know dueling is not limited merely to spells. Magical potions, powders, and other objects are used, but I will not be teaching those, I am merely your charms teacher. Well, let me teach you your first spell!"

He dissolved the golden strands he had conjured and went on to teach them the lighting charm.

"Open your books to page 8," he instructed them. "And begin by reading what Aragona has to say about the subtle magic of light."

He laughed at least fifty times during the period as he taught. After they finished reading about the theory, he demonstrated the charm, and a small ball of piercing white light flickered into existence in front of him. Then, everyone got to practice on their own. Near the end of the lesson, he drew the thick curtains closed so that the classroom was pitch black. He proceeded to choreograph a little light show with the students, each lighting and un-lighting their wands when he directed them to. The effect was very satisfying.

Ella left the classroom twenty minutes later, arm-in-arm with Selena, laughing merrily about their first lesson.

Next was Defense Against the Dark Arts with the mean wizard, Professor Tantalus. It was considerably less enjoyable than charms. Tantalus walked past Ella and Selena quite a couple of times, but he pretended not to notice them until Ella cast a spell wrong. Instead of blocking a curse, the curse went bouncing across the room, hitting Jenna, and her nose swelled unusually large.

She went to the matron, and Ella got detention three days in a row. Then, Professor Tantalus stopped controlling himself and made the same snide remarks about them as everyone else in the class.

Math made Ella scratch her head. Her mathematics education was scarce, for her parents concentrated mostly on teaching her spellwork and other magical topics. Professor Kitlowski, the teacher, had apparently seen a lot of cases like Ella and didn't go very hard on her. As he peered over her shoulder at her worksheet, he gave a dispirited little head shake and moved on.

Ella looked back at her questions, very confused. With a pang, she wished she had Charlotte back again so that she could help her.

Potions class was tough as well, though the teacher, Professor Stoddart, was an extremely kind wizard. He helped them and showed sympathy, and even though Oliver's potion was black instead of orange, he gave him good marks.

At lunch, Ella, Oliver, and Selena sat with their ham and Swiss cheese sandwiches, abusing Tantalus together. However, they were forced to stop when Herald walked past, muttering a reluctant warning.

The gym classes were great fun but extremely dangerous. Gym at Mountain View was very different from regular gym. There was a variety of sports: one was called cannonball, and played like volleyball. The main difference was the ball was very ferocious and kept zooming off in the wrong direction of its own accord. It was very dangerous, and Amy had a tooth knocked out. Professor Ventum shook her head and sent Amy to the matron.

Ella, however, was able to hit the ball five times during the lesson and avoided any accidents.

"How are you so good at it?" grumbled Selena, as she nearly had her ear taken off three times in a row.

"Ace might've had a part in it," muttered Ella. "He says any sister of his must be good at cannonball." They both burst into laughter.

Language Arts Ella liked. Professor Cleves was a plump little witch with a ruddy face. She passed out different texts and read to them the whole class with a scholarly British accent Selena took to admiring, and their homework was merely to do some comprehensive questions.

Transfiguration with Professor Iris was not very fun. The transfiguring itself was fun, but Professor Iris was strict, and she didn't laugh much. They were transfiguring a toothpick to a sewing needle today.

In the end, Ella's toothpick went silver. Though, to the touch, it was rough, so Ella knew it was still wooden. Selena and Oliver were suffering just as much, however, so she was not very dismayed.

After the class, Ella, Oliver, and Selena left the classroom together, comparing their Transfiguration results. As they were buried deep in discussion, Ella bumped head-first into Charlotte and Harry.

"Oh, I'm so sorry—!" Ella began, until she raised her head and saw Charlotte's familiar face. Ella immediately flushed scarlet.

Charlotte gasped a little, looking very troubled. "We're so sorry, Ella, we really are! We didn't want you to be in the second-tier group, you really are smart!"

"Yes!" Harry said.

"Ella," Charlotte explained. "I don't want you to drop your new friends, but we want to still be friends."

"Right!" Selena said. "Ella, isn't this what you wanted? We'll all be friends. All of us together." She looked sideways at Ella.

Ella laughed. She clutched her stomach and doubled over. Charlotte, Harry, Selena, and Oliver looked on with concern and puzzlement.

"When have I blamed you for putting me into second-tier?" wheezed Ella, still giggling. "And at which point did I mention we were no longer friends? You get silly notions. All five of us *are* friends!"

Selena beamed at her.

The next thing Ella knew, she was gasping for breath because Charlotte was on her, both arms wrapped around her chest, squeezing with all her might.

"Alright, don't suffocate her, Charlotte," Harry said with a grin.

"We have History of Magic next," Ella said when she recovered.

"We don't!" Harry grumbled.

They parted for the time being.

History of Magic could have been more enjoyable. Professor Historic was a stumpy little wizard with a bald head who was quite a good teacher, but he had a dreadful temper. A first-year boy named George Powell was apparently hard at hearing, and after being asked to repeat his question three times in a row, Professor Historic resigned to smashing the nearest ink bottle. Selena flinched, and she was positively pushing to exit the classroom first when the bell rang.

Next was dinnertime. Ella's stomach was growling, so she was very eager to get down to the Dining Hall. As they were turning into the Hall, they saw Professor Historic standing, talking to Charlotte.

Charlotte looked rather bewildered and flattered. As they walked closer, they could hear Professor Historic saying in a very nice tone, so unlike his usual one.

"And if you have any questions, any at all, my dear girl, ask me after class. I'd be glad to answer."

Professor Historic patted Charlotte's shoulder paternally, and walked off.

Charlotte caught sight of them and headed over. Just as she joined them, Penelope Brown walked passed, looking suspiciously at Charlotte.

"What was that about?" Ella asked as they looked for seats.

"He offered to help me if I have any problems in his class," Charlotte said. "That tone was so uncharacteristic of him though."

Just then, Harry found a spot and Charlotte squeezed in beside him. Ella waved a small goodbye, as they were forced to sit at different tables.

Dinner was tasty, with beef stew and baked potatoes. After dinner, however, during the long period until Astro-mag at midnight, they all went to the library to start on their already massive pile of homework. But their time in the library was cut short, for the weather was so great outside, they went out to enjoy it. Charlotte, putting studying above everything, took her books outside to work in the grass.

Selena lay down on the grass under the sun. She crossed her feet and spread out her arms. The smell of fresh pine needles and their sweet-smelling sap filled the air, it was so strong that it covered the scent of smoke. The lake glistened under the afternoon sun, and the sound of splashing water could be heard as students went swimming.

"It's so good to be in a place that isn't infested with smoke for a change," she breathed contentedly.

"Yeah," said Oliver. "Do you reckon it's the magical protection on the school or is it just because of geographic reasons?"

"What is the most important element in moonstone again?" Charlotte asked, scratching her chin with her quill absent-mindedly.

"I think it is iron," Selena replied.

"You don't know that, Lexington?" came a cold voice. "Why, I don't feel like you have the talent to be with the intellectually gifted students, like me!"

Ella, Charlotte, Selena, Harry, and Oliver whirled around.

Penelope Brown was in a tree, accompanied by Sam and Bob.

"It's not up to you to decide which group Charlotte's in!" Ella retorted.

"Oh yeah? Who are you? Oh, right—Ross, and, ah—the Snow boy," Penelope said.

"So what?" Oliver shot.

She frowned.

"Enjoy your privacy, Ross, Hayfield, and Caroline. Soon enough, it'll be gone," She turned, and her robes swept the ground as she led Sam and Bob back into the building.

"Enjoy our privacy? It'll soon be gone? What's she going on about?" Selena asked quizzically, glaring after Penelope's swinging braids.

SEVEN

The Dungeon of Unknown Doom

"That's really suspicious, you know," Charlotte said, staring after Penelope in puzzlement. "I wonder what she means."

"She's acting strange, even for Penelope Brown," Ella told her.

"Honestly, Charlotte, I think we better take it to the authorities," Harry told her, scooting forward. "This is getting really strange... wildfires, strange symbols, suspicious people... "

"Agreed," Charlotte stood up. "We better go to Professor Watonburn."

"Wait, why?" Ella stood up in surprise.

"You heard Harry, we have to tell someone all the strange things going on, I doubt they're completely random."

"Alright, but this is so sudden, Charlotte and Harry had a revelation and now we're off to see the Headmaster in a matter of seconds for literally no reason?"

"Not no reason, just come!" Charlotte said, exasperated.

"I'm not coming," said Ella. "I don't want to get in trouble!"

"Ella, please." Charlotte grabbed her hand. "Come on, trust me, this will be worth it."

So, they went into the building and stared at the long entrance hall that stretched in front of them, ending at the large oak wood doors that led into the Dining hall. Along the corridor, there were ten doors, five on each side.

"Where is his office?" asked Charlotte.

"No idea, we'll have to search the entire school, probably," Harry replied.

None of the doors in the entrance corridor led to his office, so they climbed the steps to the second story, and the door wasn't there either. It also wasn't on the third, fourth, or fifth floors.

"Um, we should try the towers, since there are no more floors to check," Charlotte suggested.

They ventured up to the east tower and then the west, but his office wasn't there. Nor was it in the north or south towers.

"There is only one place left," said Harry, panting hard. "The High Tower."

The High Tower was forbidden for students to wander in, but they knew they weren't wandering – or at least everyone but Ella did – so they felt safe going up the steps.

When they reached the top of the stairs, they knew that this was it. It was a circular room filled with about thirty doors. When they walked past the doors, they found that they were labeled each with a teacher's name. Directly across from them were a pair of large marble doors similar to the ones leading to the dining hall. Golden letters were engraved on the slabs of stone: **PROFESSOR HELIOS WATONBURN**.

They walked across the floor, and just as Ella was raising her hand to knock, a dangerously soft voice sounded. "Lexington, Ross, Caroline, Hayfield, Snow. Such a big group of students to put in detention!"

They whirled around to find Professor Tantalus, smirking.

"I expect you know that this tower is out of bounds for students!"

"Professor Tantalus, we aren't wandering!" said Ella.

"If you aren't wandering, what are you doing, you mediocre child?" he asked.

"We are here on important business," Harry informed him.

"I didn't ask you, you little shrimp," Professor Tantalus said softly. "And I doubt anyone of your sad intellect could have anything important on his mind."

"But Harry is in first-tier!" Selena said softly.

"Does it look like I care?" Tantalus asked her. "And if any one of you talk back to me again, I shall suspend you. Show-off."

Selena blushed, but just then, the door behind them opened, and Professor Watonburn was standing there.

"Have we got a problem?" he asked calmly. "Because, if so, I would most like to resolve it, as arguing is distracting for me when I am working," He smiled softly.

"Of course, there is a problem!" said Professor Tantalus. "These students are wandering in this tower! I have learned extremely quickly that they have zero regard for rules whatsoever, two nights they have been here, and twice I have caught them out of bed when they were not supposed to be."

Professor Watonburn looked at them.

"I believe they have something important yet urgent to tell me, Ivan. I do not believe they are wandering. Please let me deal with them."

Professor Watonburn nodded at the fuming Professor Tantalus, and he steered all five of them into his study.

"Professor, well, we were in—"

"Not now, Ella. Wait until we're in the private part of my study," Professor Watonburn said and gave Ella quite a shock. No teacher yet had called them by their first names.

Through the big wooden doors, there was a circular room filled with chairs. A big wooden table stood before them, and there was a cushioned chair behind it.

"Ah, this is my conference room," Professor Watonburn said. "It is open to the public, so we must go deeper into the concealed area."

Behind the cushioned chair, there was a portrait of Mountain View from the outside. Professor Watonburn yelled to it, "Ram horns!" The portrait fell off the wall and dropped onto the floor. He stepped through and beckoned them in.

Just as Ella was about to go through, she heard it again. A faint rustle. It sounded much closer now and somehow seemed like the rustle of robes. Ella told herself she probably imagined it because the only other thing it could be was the wind.

"Ella, you coming?" asked Harry.

"Oh, yeah. I'm coming," She turned her back on it and stepped into the private study.

It was a cozy place. A fire roared in the far end of the room, almost fully concealed by the chair and desk in front of it. A velvet rug lay in the center of the room, woven with complicated patterns. Besides that, interesting wooden chests of all shapes and sizes were scattered around the edge of the circular room.

"Very well. Have a seat," said Professor Watonburn, flicking his wand. Suddenly, five chintz armchairs appeared before his desk, and they each sat on one of them.

Rustle, rustle...

Ella turned her head so fast she almost broke her neck. There was nothing, no one. Rubbing her neck, she turned to face Professor Watonburn again.

"So, I hear you have something to tell me?" he asked courteously.

"Yes," said Ella. "We were on the grounds a little earlier, and then Penelope Brown showed up."

Professor Watonburn nodded.

"She told Selena, Oliver, and I to enjoy our privacy, because, before long, she said it'd be gone," Ella continued. "So, Charlotte and Harry, being first-tiers, thought it was suspicious and it's not an isolated incident, so we came here to you."

Charlotte blushed and smiled a little, trying not to look pleased with herself.

"I see," said Professor Watonburn. "I will talk to her later. Is there anything else?"

"Ella, it's not about what tier you're in," Charlotte assured her. "It's something else. Professor, you see, nobody can deny it's all been very strange, the abundance of wildfires. And, there's this mark that shot out of my wand at Vandenberg's, when I was getting a wand—!"

"I know," Professor Watonburn said quietly.

Charlotte stopped mid-sentence. "What do you mean?"

"Charlotte, it's high time I told you," Professor Watonburn leaned forward and rested his elbows on the desk. "You are sharp, and you are right. They are not at all isolated incidents."

Charlotte gasped, and looked around meaningfully at her friends.

They looked equally shocked.

"The mark from your wand at Vandenberg's, it is the mark of the Dungeon of Unknown Doom. Dear Vandenberg messaged me as soon as you'd left his shop."

"Sir, what is the Dungeon of—?" Charlotte started.

"The Dungeon is one of the creations of the dark witch, Dagina."

At these words, Ella, Selena, and Harry both started in surprise. Ella breathed, "No way!" and Selena clapped her hand to her mouth.

"Dagina?" Oliver asked, quizzically.

"Of course, you would not know," Professor Watonburn continued calmly. "Dagina, or to use her real name, Jessica Aphelion, was the worst tyrant the magical world has ever seen. She is a dark, evil witch, who specializes in the dark arts.

"Her first reported sighting was in the fourth century, in Pella, Greece. Her first evil doing was recorded in the form of the Katadesmoi, what was somewhat common in those days. It translates to a curse tablet, which is essentially its function. It carries a curse, and it would be buried with the dead, hoping the spirit would communicate the desired curse to the gods of the underworld.

"In the tablet, she wished to destroy the thing that caused her pain—you shall not need to know, but I'm sure you will learn in due course—and it did not work. Because the gods of the underworld were not real. Since then, Dagina has been relentless in her search for true curses, which is what ultimately led her to the dark side."

He paused a moment, looking mournfully at each of them in turn. Ella shifted in her seat, and Professor Watonburn continued on.

"She has seemingly discovered the secret to immortality, because she has popped up all over the centuries, and is allegedly still alive now. She has periods in which she hid, not revealing herself to the public. Sometimes, she would disappear for centuries. Some people would think she had finally gone, but she kept reappearing.

"One of Dagina's worst acts was her creation of the Dungeon of Unknown Doom. It is rumored to be hidden in these very Rocky Mountains, and it's supposed to house dangerous beasts and dark spells.

"The concept is self-explanatory. If anybody wanders in, they are subject to the 'doom' in the Dungeon. She created it as a trap for unsuspecting victims. The Dungeon has claimed the lives of hundreds over the years.

"It also allows people with dark intentions to enter, without suffering the fate of doom.

"But there was a flaw in her spell. It has been found the Dungeon does not like being forced to hold dark magic. It occasionally chooses the worthy to destroy it. And that symbol from your wand, Charlotte, that's the symbol of the Dungeon of Unknown Doom. You see now, you were destined to destroy it."

A ringing silence fell.

"Me?" Charlotte breathed.

Professor Watonburn nodded encouragingly and nodded.

"And the wildfires—?"

"They're likely to be connected to the Dungeon as well," Professor Watonburn confirmed.

Charlotte bit her tongue and looked sideways at Ella. She gave her a small nod.

"You're... the Chosen One," Oliver told Charlotte.

Suddenly, Charlotte laughed.

"Professor," she smiled. "I'm just a kid, I'm barely nine, I don't know anything about magic. How could I possibly have been chosen?"

"And that... is the mystery," Professor Watonburn smiled at her. "But it is evident, there are qualities in you that the Dungeon values. Well, I have kept you long enough, you should be off, if there is nothing else," Professor Watonburn said.

Ella thought about telling him about the rustling noise, but she felt it was not worthy.

"Sam Corps and Bob Vodvanov," Ella finally said.

"Excuse me?" said Professor Watonburn.

"Penelope is almost always in the company of Sam Corps and Bob Vodvanov," Ella explained. "I think they're in the same boat."

Professor Watonburn nodded absentmindedly. He was staring into space, deep in thought.

Finally, he looked back at her and said, "I knew Mrs. Corps and Mrs. Vodvanov. They were sisters who attended Mountain View. I taught them!" Ella gasped. "I was Charms teacher back then." Professor Watonburn continued. "They seemed to have a strange obsession for learning dark magic."

They all gasped once more.

Professor Watonburn nodded. "I'll talk to all three, Penelope, Bob, and Sam, and their parents," he said, "but I can't guarantee an honest answer. If that is all, you may leave."

"But Professor, how could Penelope know I was chosen? How could she learn about that?" Charlotte asked.

"Remember, her family runs deep in the dark arts," Professor Watonburn replied gravely. "She is sharp, too, she catches details others don't. Now, you must really be off."

Ella nodded, and she stood up. The other four followed suit. Professor Watonburn accompanied them to the door.

"But promise me," he was saying, "not to mention any of this to anyone."

"We promise," Ella said.

Rustle. Rustle. Rustle.

"That sound!" she shouted, turning towards the door. She knew she was silly because no one was there.

"Excuse me?" repeated Professor Watonburn.

"Sorry, sorry. It was nothing," Ella said. So, with a wave of goodbye to Professor Watonburn, she and her friends walked back down the tower.

"What sound?" asked Charlotte when they were walking down.

"I said it is nothing! It's probably the wind!" Ella said shortly and quickly. She didn't want to appear to be having hallucinations, so she didn't tell them.

Instead, she changed the subject. "Can you believe it?" she asked. "We got Penelope!"

EIGHT

Tests and Truths

They chatted happily as they went back to the library. If Charlotte was troubled that the fate of thousands of Coloradoans were upon her shoulders, she did not show it.

There was no point going outside, the sun was almost setting.

They managed to get Sparks' and Tantalus' work done, with time ticking by and midnight being only ten minutes away.

Ella said, "I actually can't believe we got so much done. According to Ace, it was supposed to take forever," she laughed.

The Astro-magic class took place on top of the roof where it was freezing cold during the night. They were at the North Tower because they were learning about the North Star. The good thing about this course was that finally, all five of them were together, for they had all chosen this elective.

After half an hour of tedious stargazing, Professor Celeste narrating about the different stars in the background, they were frozen nearly numb. It was all very well for Professor Celeste, for she was evidently prepared, having worn a thick midnight-blue cloak with little star sequins sown in, but the rest of them were shivering in their shirts. Harry redid his tie around his head like a scarf in an effort to keep warm.

Finally, the period was up, and they were sent off the roof with a note that they were going to the East Tower next class to study the heavens from a different angle.

"Remind me," grumbled Oliver, as he and Ella and Selena sat around their common room fire before bed. "Remind me, "next time to wear the uniform sweater and cloak to Astro-mag. I don't care if they're winter garments, it's so cold."

"If this is what it's like in fall," muttered Ella. "I shiver to think about the winter nights."

"Kind of hard to shiver just now though," Selena smiled, warming her hands by the flames.

As Ella and Selena finally got into bed, Selena muttered, "I'm so sleepy!" Ella, full of sleepiness and happiness, fell asleep in no time, too.

The next morning, they met Charlotte and Harry at breakfast.

The day went smoothly, and the second-tiers had their first Herbology and History of Magic classes.

In Herbology, Professor Rose taught them the different magical plant categories. In short, all magical plants were divided into either practical or oriental. Practical plants were plants that had magical properties or those that were common in potion-making and medicine-mixing. Oriental plants were merely for show. After that, both categories were divided into water plants and land plants, then trees, shrubs, grass, or flowers.

In History of Magic, Professor Historic gave them a basic rundown of all Wizarding history in one hour. He was a dramatic storyteller, and Ella very much enjoyed his class. Though his talks were brief today, it was enough for Ella to appreciate how interesting this class would be.

None of them had Astro-mag that night, but Ella had to leave at six o'clock for her detention with Professor Tantalus.

"This is going to be a nightmare!" complained Ella. "And I have to do the same tomorrow and the day after that!"

They studied until eleven (taking advantage of being away from home and the late curfew, for the older students had *a lot* of homework), and Ella came back just as they were packing to leave.

"How was it?" asked Charlotte.

"Terrible," answered Ella. "He made me clean the Dungeon floors!"

Besides that, the first week went perfectly, and just as they were about to retire for the weekend, Katherine the Prefect hurried towards them.

"Have you not got the message yet?" she asked urgently.

"No, what message?" asked Ella.

"All of you must go to the auditorium!" she cried. "Hurry!"

She led them to the third floor and into the dark auditorium. They found seats at the back, and as they sat down, the lights went on above the stage.

Everyone quieted down. The curtains opened, and Professor Austin stood there.

"Hello, students. It is probably way too early in the year to get your mind cranked, but, as a friendly reminder, I must tell you that your end-of-year examinations are quite important."

Many older students groaned loudly, and Professor Austin glared at them and continued.

"If you would not like to listen to me," she said sternly, "Then you might as well get a T on your tests."

She looked around at the audience.

A tiny first-year boy raised his hand nervously. Ella recognized him as George Powell, the boy Professor Historic had shouted at the previous day.

"Professor," he said. "What is a 'T'?"

Penelope smirked and commented loudly two rows behind them, "Doesn't even know what's a *T*! He seems thick enough to actually get one! For your information, Mr. Powell, I understand the non-magical schools grade from A to F, but here at Mountain View we grade with O, E, A, P, D, and T. They respectively stand for outstanding, exceeds expectations, acceptable, poor, dreadful, and troll."

George nodded in acknowledgment and sat back down, a bit bewildered, though smiling at his friends like he just did something very impressive.

Another first-year girl also raised her hand.

"Ashley?"

"Professor, not to be rude, but what's your job?" Ashley asked, with her head bowed low with embarrassment. "You are a professor, but

I've never been to your classes."

"For that, Ashley, I am an extra tutor, counselor, and deputy headmistress at this school," Professor Austin replied. "But such questions are off-topic. About the exams?"

Ashley sat back down, and Professor Austin waited. When no more hands went up, she continued her speech.

"These tests matter very much to your future. If you think you have more important tests in the future to prove you are intelligent enough to embark on your career, you are wrong. Every employer looks at his employee's entire exam history from Mountain View. Please take care. Also, I will be giving Prefects leaflets to pass around in their group. They will contain career advice and such."

She went backstage to put down the parchment.

"Now," she said when she came back, "you are dismissed. But, Miss Charlotte Lexington and Penelope Brown, please come to the stage."

A loud shuffling started as students began clearing out of the auditorium. Charlotte stood up and started winding her way through the mountains of people. When she had finally pushed her way to the stage, her friends following close behind her, Professor Watonburn was there too.

He was looking stern. "Thank you, Athena." He nodded, and Professor Austin retreated into the shadows.

A few moments later, Penelope emerged from the crowd, flanked as usual by Sam and Bob.

"Hello," Professor Watonburn smiled, no longer that stern. "Miss Penelope Venus Brown, I heard some very interesting things recently. I know you are sharp and must've found out. Tell me, what do you plan regarding the Dungeon of Unknown Doom?"

Ella put her hand over her mouth, hiding a wide grin. So did Harry and Oliver. Charlotte and Selena bit their lips.

"And your friends, Sam Corps and Bob Vodvanov."

Penelope looked both angry and puzzled while Sam and Bob sat dumbly, staring into space.

"Good acting!" Harry snickered.

Professor Watonburn continued to look intently at her.

"Is it true that a clearly intelligent first year like you is planning something quite dangerous and ambitious?" he asked.

Penelope frowned. "I don't understand."

"I'm afraid you do."

"Well, I don't think I am?"

"I want a very certain and straightforward answer," Professor Watonburn was saying.

"Well, we're not saying!" Penelope exploded.

Professor Watonburn looked quite taken aback, but he understood. He nodded slowly.

"Of course," he said. "I can always cast a truth spell," Penelope gasped as he said this. "But then, I have no right to invade your privacy, so I won't use it, especially in front of everyone. My only goal was to make sure you are aware of the horrors running around, and I beg you not to mess with it. I'll be talking to your parents, Penelope," said Professor Watonburn. "As well as yours, Sam and Bob."

He nodded to Penelope, who quickly turned and left the stage.

Harry and Oliver frowned and groaned. "He should have done it!" Harry muttered under his breath.

Professor Watonburn now turned to Charlotte and her friends. "I understand if you do not want to take such risks," he said. "But if you *are* willing to, please do destroy the Dungeon."

"Why can't you do it, sir?" asked Ella.

"I can only give you advice," he replied. "The Dungeon chose Charlotte."

He swept offstage and walked towards the stairs.

"Professor Austin?" Ella asked. "Could you—"

"No," she replied firmly. "But remember what the girl, Ashley had asked. I am the counselor and magical tutor here. Please, come to me if you need anything."

She smiled warmly for a moment, and she too swept offstage.

"We'll work on it, Ella," said Charlotte, comfortably. "We'll find a way to destroy it."

But they didn't do anything that weekend when it came to the Dungeon. The only thing they managed to do was get most of their homework done by Saturday and go for a hike out in the Rockies.

They set out at midday, carrying water bottles, jackets, and snacks in their packs. They hitched a ride in one of the Waterside carriages that brought them to the school. Without a definite destination in mind, they let the Pegasi fly them above the grey-green earthy landscape until they touched down beside a circular lake.

Charlotte, reading a map, looked up and informed them that they were at Lily Lake, close to Jurassic Park.

"What? Let me see," retorted Oliver at this news.

"I'm telling you, it's called Jurassic Park!" Charlotte insisted. "It's a rock-climbing destination, there are these really cool springs at the top, we ought to take a look."

"Fine, but if we encounter dinosaurs, what will we do?"

Charlotte ignored this led them up the mountain. It was steep and without a path. They trudged along, kicking up dirt and gravel. Charlotte and Harry went ahead and scouted the best way up. Bending low and utilizing their hands to keep balance, the five of them climbed upwards, between the coniferous trees.

Unusually, there were more tree stumps than full-grown trees here. Ella, who had camped before in these very mountains, did not understand why all the trees had been felled. She turned to point this out to Charlotte.

"It's because of the wildfires," Charlotte told her. "People are cutting down trees so there would be less timber to burn if the fires come through. It's for wildfire prevention."

"Almost there," panted Harry.

Just then, a cry sounded behind them. Ella had stepped on a rock, and it become dislodged under her weight. She hopped lightly off.

"Careful," said Oliver.

Soon enough, they had toiled to the top. The wind howled ferociously, whipping their jackets around them and biting their skin. It whistled and Oliver felt it sounded rather like a creature roaring. He kept glancing around nervously for dinosaurs as Charlotte showed them two enormous craters in the rock, which were filled with green water.

"Doesn't look like a place for a swim," Harry commented.

Oliver threw a rock inside. It rippled on the surface and disappeared. "Is it deep?"

"You're not actually thinking of trying?" Selena gasped.

Oliver shrugged mischievously.

The five of them mainly crowded around the right-hand one, since it was considerably larger and the closest. Ella strayed over to peer at the left one, but nobody else paid it much attention.

"Ella, you coming?" Charlotte's voice called as she bent over the water, which was deeper, darker, and admittedly rather foul-smelling.

There was no greenery up here, only bare rock. Penelope found a cavity in the rock that formed a kind of seat. She sat down joyfully, as if it were a throne.

After some sightseeing, they found an area sheltered from the wind and had a small picnic snack break. After that, the sun was sinking. Charlotte led them down the mountain the same way they came.

"Tighten your boots before we go," Charlotte advised them. "I once read in a hiking pamphlet that if you don't, when you descend, your toes will repeatedly collide with the front of your boot, hurting your feet."

Harry snickered at this a little, but they all consented to re-lacing their hiking boots before starting the downward trek.

They took the journey back. By the time they reached the gates, dusk was settling in, and they were all exhausted. They were all glad to reach the warmth and comfort of the dining hall, heaping platters of delicious food in front of them.

After dinner, they went back to the library to finish a bit of last-minute work.

"I'm so tired," yawned Oliver, rubbing his eyes resignedly as he attempted to read a text on stirring technique for potions. "My mind keeps drifting, I am hearing the words but not taking in the meaning. Should we retire for the night?"

"Can't," groaned Harry. "If we don't read this bit tonight, we're going to be behind in class tomorrow."

Charlotte wasn't complaining. She finished her homework before the hike was now buried deep in a book.

"What're you reading?" asked Harry curiously after taking notes on the three different stirring techniques used in Potions.

"Nothing!" snapped Charlotte as she tugged the book away.

"It's something, Charlotte," He took the book from her and looked at the cover.

"*Your First Guide to Fighting Dark Magic*? Do you think we'll be able to find something for the Dungeon in a beginner book?"

"I can't find anything more difficult that isn't restricted for first-years," Charlotte sighed.

"Let me see."

Harry wandered over to the restricted area and pulled off a book called *Break Hard and Dark Charms*. He took it back and set in on the table as Professor Boock ran over.

"Your note," Professor Boock said simply.

"Huh?" asked Harry.

"If you want to take a book from the restricted section, you must have a note of permission from a teacher," she said.

"Oh," Harry looked down at the book.

"No note, no book!" she said strictly, taking the book and replacing it on the shelf.

Harry sighed.

"See?" said Charlotte, going to the return bin and taking out the book again.

Harry sighed again.

NINE

Penelope Brown

Three weeks later, it became evident that Monday was the worst day of the week. In addition to the regular back-to-work blues, they had to be up at midnight for Astro-mag, which proved duller with each lesson. They were making star charts now in class, which was slow and dreary work. Harry had had enough of it after four lessons.

"I can't figure anything out!" complained Harry, massaging his forehead. "I've got a headache from this!"

He indicated the pile of scrapped parchment, protractors, and calculations in front of him. Charlotte gave a little *tut-tut* and leaned forward to examine his work.

"You have made a miscalculation," she informed him. "Fifty-six point five plus seventy-nine point eight equals one hundred and thirty-six point three, not one hundred and twenty-five. This means your angle is off about eleven degrees. If you edit your line—" Charlotte took out a quill and began redrawing Harry's Orion constellation "—you get... Pollux!"

"You're a wonder," Harry shook his head as he pinpointed the star Pollux on his chart according to Charlotte's calculations.

Monday afternoon, they were working outside again. Selena and Charlotte were exempted from potions homework, for their last Attentiveness Draughts were reportedly so effective that their test subjects (everyone got a gerbil) stared at Professor Stoddart unblinkingly for seven hours in a row.

Charlotte was reading again, and Selena was polishing her wand with a rag.

"What's this?" Selena asked as she began cleaning the tip of her wand.

"Hm?" asked Charlotte, raising her head from her book and looking over.

"There are some scratches here," Selena pointed out. "But I've been very careful with it."

"Accidents happen," grumbled Harry, as he flipped open potion books, researching the properties of unicorn horn. He had somehow exploded his cauldron during the same potions class that Charlotte and Selena excelled in. Professor Stoddart analyzed his work and told him he had used far too liberal amounts of unicorn horn, and told him his homework was to research its properties and uses in potion-making.

"Don't worry Harry," said Charlotte soothingly. "It was a very difficult lesson. Back in the 1700s, they didn't teach Attentiveness Draughts until second-year!"

"Let me see, Selena," Ella scooted over by Selena. Selena handed her the wand, and Ella held it up to the sun, examining it.

"It sure looks like a scratch," said Ella quizzically. "Almost like somebody shaved a patch off."

"Who would do that?" asked Oliver skeptically. "More likely it got banged up somewhere."

That's when Penelope arrived.

"Get away from us, blunder-head, or we'll get you expelled!" shouted Harry.

"Oh, yes, very clever!" she smirked.

"Oh yeah, cleverer than you'd ever be in a million years!" shouted Selena.

Penelope walked towards them.

"Oh, sure," she said. "Try it, Caroline. You'll know," Penelope turned away and into the school.

"Not Professor Watonburn again?" asked Ella.

"Yes," said Charlotte, "but briefly. I'll go alone," She sprinted up the steps as Ella watched her disappear into the entrance corridor.

She sprinted up to the high tower, panting. She knocked. The door swung inwards immediately, as if he had been expecting her. Professor Watonburn was signing letters on his desk.

"Oh, um, sorry! I...anyway, um...sorry, I..." Charlotte mumbled.

"Oh no!" said Professor Watonburn. "How may I help you, Charlotte?" He shoved the papers aside and looked up expectantly.

"I would just like a written note from you to access the restricted area in the library," she said. "To research on the Dungeon."

"Oh, yes!" Professor Watonburn said, taking out a strip of parchment. It read:

I, Professor Watonburn, henceforth give permission to Charlotte Lexington and her friends to look in the restricted area to research the Dungeon of Unknown Doom.

He handed the note to Charlotte and said, "I'm sorry I haven't done this before, I was considering the more gruesome texts in the restricted section. Good luck!" Charlotte nodded, thanked him, ran out of the room, and dashed back to her friends.

"Got it, let's go!" she said breathlessly, pulling on her pack.

"Got what? Go where?" asked Ella hurriedly.

"I just got...a note of...permission from...Professor Watonburn...to visit the restricted...area, let's go...to the library!" she panted as she ran into the school.

As they turned to go up the stairs to the library, they met Professor Iris. She was carrying a large stack of papers, and the uppermost sheets all blew off the stack as they zoomed past her.

"Slow down!" she yelled after them. "Avoid running in the corridors if you can help it!"

"Sorry!" Ella yelled back as they rounded the stairs.

In the library, Charlotte dashed up to Professor Boock and panted loudly. "Here...note for accessing...the restricted...area!"

"Quiet, quiet!" she hissed as she examined the paper. She held it up to the light as if to detect a forgery.

Finally, she smoothed out the parchment and locked it in a drawer filled with notes. "Okay," she muttered, turning away. "Look as much as you want."

Charlotte went and got *Break Hard and Dark Charms* again and started reading.

"Hello there."

They whipped around. It, of course, was Penelope.

"What're you doing here?" hissed Oliver.

"None of your business, Hayfield," She beckoned to Sam and Bob and walked across the library to the restricted section and pulled out a dusty, molding book.

Harry glanced at Professor Boock. She was replacing books on the shelves. She saw Penelope taking the book and nodded at her.

Penelope returned with the book and sat in front of them, setting the text on the table. Ella caught a glimpse of its leather-bound cover before Penelope flipped it open: *Potions and Poisons*. Ella frowned.

"Never witnessed a teacher being nice to you? Oh geez, that Stoddart is just too *sympathetic*." She said the word exactly how someone would have said *disgusting*. Then she smirked. "Hate him. Father says people should only be nice to ones that have proven themselves worthy, and of course, you guys haven't."

"And what does your father do?" asked Oliver. "Examine dragon dung?" Ella suppressed a giggle.

"Well, as you see," said Penelope, frowning. "He works for the Congress of Magic, and I dare say it's a way better job than your father's, Ross. Doesn't your father run a business in—ah, Hermes Plaza? Why, father's one week salary would mean an absolute fortune to your father, Ross!" She smirked.

Harry and Selena burst up from their seats.

"I might as well duel you if it's the last thing I do!" shouted Selena.

"These days, all you've been going on about is how good you and your family are, but you might as well be a criminal once we cast a truth charm on you and destroy the Dungeon!" roared Harry.

"Honestly! Is this a library or a playground?" asked Professor Boock, hurrying over. "Detention, you two!" Everyone was staring at Harry and Selena curiously.

Selena was looking at Professor Boock's figure moving along the aisles with an *are-you-serious-she-provoked-us-I'm-disgusted* look.

Harry was glaring at the smirking Penelope, and both of them were still standing.

"Sit down, everyone's looking at us!" whispered a worried Charlotte, tugging on Harry's sleeve.

"You too, Selena!" whispered Ella.

Hesitantly, Harry sat down. Selena followed suit. Ella looked around nervously and buried her face in her backpack, pretending to look for something. Everyone was still looking at them. Embarrassed, Ella whispered, "Let's work somewhere else."

Penelope, seeing they were leaving, beckoned to Sam and Bob, and they too packed and followed them out of the library. "Hey, Caroline!" Penelope yelled.

Selena turned around. "What now?" she shouted.

Penelope frowned and came closer. "'I might as well duel you if it is the last thing I do!' Well, let's do it then."

Selena frowned.

"Tomorrow afternoon, right after lessons."

"Oh, sure! And you'll lose before you could mutter a single incantation!" shouted Oliver.

"No!" screamed Charlotte. She grabbed hold of Oliver's sleeve right as he was about to charge at Penelope. "Don't!"

Penelope smirked. "Then is the duel still on?" she asked scathingly.

"No," said Charlotte firmly, leaving the job of restraining Oliver to Ella. "No."

"Charlotte!" moaned Harry. "We'll win if you have any doubts!" However, Charlotte ignored him.

"I know you are trying to provoke him into doing something wrong," said Charlotte.

"Charlotte, there's nothing wrong with—!" Harry stopped after receiving a glare from Charlotte.

"In case you haven't read the four-foot-long list of rules posted in the library thoroughly, it says any unauthorized dueling is prohibited," she explained simply as Penelope's smirk was wiped off her face. "Now, if you doesn't have anything else to say, I'd think we'd better go."

She turned around and led them away from Penelope, and she

could've sworn she heard Penelope saying, "Ugh, such a goody-two-shoes."

Charlotte frowned. She whirled around. "Do you really want to duel, now?" she asked curiously. "Because I can help you if you *really* want to duel."

Penelope swung her hair. "Anything to get rid of you old bats."

"Tomorrow afternoon, right after lessons then." Charlotte smiled and ran off.

"Huh?" said Harry.

"Come on!" yelled Charlotte exuberantly, and she dashed to Professor Sparks's office.

She rapped on the door. "Come in!" came a muffled voice.

Charlotte pushed open the door and stepped in. "Professor?" she said softly. "We were wondering about the dueling club. Could we join?" she asked.

Professor Sparks took off his glasses and surveyed her thoughtfully. "Yes," he decided, and thrust some papers at her with a small smile. "Sign up."

Charlotte handed them each a paper and a quill, and they filled out the forms.

"Oh yeah," said Charlotte as they were turning to leave. "Our, um, *friend* also wants to join. Is it okay if we take her a sheet?" she asked.

Professor Sparks nodded absentmindedly and thrust another form towards her, and they turned to leave.

"Amazing!" said Oliver when they left the office. "Where did you find out about the dueling club?"

"The two-foot-long list of clubs posted in the library," she said agitatedly. She turned to Selena. "Go find Penelope and tell her about this," she told her, "but don't start shouting again. We'll be down by the lake."

Selena skipped away.

"Let's take a break from working since most of our homework is already finished," Charlotte said. "We can cool down by the lake and read that book."

They sat down by the water, showering themselves with droplets for a while. Once they cooled down, Charlotte pulled the book out from her pack and began reading.

After what seemed like thirty whole minutes, Selena returned.

"What kept you?" asked Ella.

"Penelope," Selena panted. "She was in the Top-tier common room, and I didn't know how to get in. I tried to force my way in, but I got caught by Penelope, and she threatened to report me. I gave it to her in the end. She was disgusted that we forgot her cronies."

She joined them and sat by the beach, showering herself with droplets also. "Anything useful in the book?" She glanced at Charlotte.

"Not that she's telling us about," said Ella.

"Hey!" Charlotte jumped up.

"What?" asked Oliver, snatching away the book before it fell in the water.

"*The Dungeon of Unknown Doom?*" he reread. "There's actually an entire chapter devoted to this!" Everyone grouped closer.

"*The Dungeon of Unknown Doom is a highly dangerous dark place. It makes the person who enters meet doom. It is still unclear exactly what magic is inside the Dungeon, although some are reports it contains a dragon.*"

"Dragons?" squeaked Ella in fright.

"*Besides fire-breathing beasts, it is likely the Dungeon contains other obstacles as well, designed to trap you and wear you down both physically and emotionally,*" Selena read on. "Doesn't sound good, does it?"

They had a good Tuesday, and that afternoon, Charlotte said, "The dueling club is open this afternoon. It's time to face Penelope, guys!"

They headed to the dueling room, and they saw Penelope waiting for them. Professor Sparks was waiting for them also.

"Three people on each side!" he called. "Pick the first, second, and third."

"Huh?" asked Oliver.

"The first is the person dueling," whispered Charlotte as they picked out some dueling robes. "The second is there to take over when the first loses or dies, but of course, the latter won't happen here. The third is to back up your side after the second dies."

She found a decent pair of leather shoes and slipped them on. She pulled a rag out of a box and polished her wand. She flicked it repeatedly before finally saying, "I'm first."

"I'm second!" shouted an exuberant Harry.

"I'm your third," said Selena.

"Aw!" Oliver complained. "What about me?"

"Hey, we'll be the audience!" Ella said. "That'll save us from any injuries."

"Penelope's got her cronies ready," observed Selena. "She's whispering to them."

Penelope was indeed whispering at them. She was standing in one lane and was whispering hurriedly to Sam and Bob. Oliver frowned and edged closer, trying to eavesdrop.

"And if you need to take over, Sam," she was whispering. "Disarm them first."

"All right?" asked Charlotte, drawing a deep breath. "Okay, let's go!" She stood at the other side of the lane, while Harry and Selena stood behind her. Ella and Oliver waited tensely on the benches, clapping and shouting words of encouragement.

"Scared, Lexington? Feeling regretful?" crooned a smirking Penelope. "I'll let you surrender!"

"Never!" Charlotte muttered through clenched teeth.

"Lose or surrender, Lexington? Because I am—argh!" Charlotte had aimed her wand at Penelope and willed her to be thrown backward.

Professor Sparks hurried over. "You all right?" she asked. "It was a good, strong hex, I must say!" He surveyed Charlotte cheerily before helping Penelope up. "Go to Madame McGrant." He indicated the matron that was hurriedly mending someone's bruise.

Penelope staggered up to her feet and glared white-hot at Charlotte before going.

Sam dumbly replaced her, and slowly waved his wand. "Fl-fla-flame—!"

Charlotte sent a spell at him to make him double over.

Sam managed to block the curse, and it bounded across the room, where it struck a portrait of a famous dueler and set it on fire. Sam stared at Professor Sparks as he ran over to extinguish the flames.

"Slash!" Charlotte yelled.

A deep gash appeared on Sam's chest, and he fell to the ground. Madame McGrant rushed over and whispered something while gently waving her wand. Without saying anything, she lifted him off the floor and took him to a bed.

"Nice!" whispered Harry.

Charlotte grinned.

"Flame!"

"Argh!"

A white-hot tongue of flame licked Charlotte's cheek. She cried out and lifted her hands to her face. The sleeves of her robes caught fire and flickered up her arm. Charlotte dropped to the ground, abandoning all pretense, and rolled over, patting out the flames on her robes.

"This group should be dismissed!" muttered McGrant, rushing over for the third time. She helped Charlotte to the other end of the room and gave her some pain-relieving potion, the same one Mr. Ross had given her after she entered Hermes Plaza. Meanwhile, McGrant dabbed a thick green liquid onto Charlotte's burn, which stung and smoked, but slowly healed the skin.

Harry bit his lip and took Charlotte's spot.

"Maximum Light!"

A jet of bright white light shot across the room and into now Bob's eyes. He shrieked and covered his eyes from the bright light, stumbling backward and tripping over the carpet.

"They react too slowly," grinned Harry.

"Amazing!" Ella ran over, followed by Oliver. "You beat them like cockroaches!"

"Yup! Hip, hip, hooray!" Harry shouted.

Selena nodded happily. "I didn't get a turn, but it's good we won!"

"Great! That was really simple, though, I'd like a bit more of a challenge!" Charlotte shouted, bounding out of bed happily, sprinting to their side. "Congrats!"

McGrant came chasing after her, pills flying out of her pocket, and her potion slopping over the side of the vial and onto the rich carpet.

Harry laughed at her. "Oh my goodness!" he said. Charlotte impatiently waved McGrant away, and they headed out of the room.

"Can't wait to see Penelope tomorrow!" sang Ella in a sing-song voice. "I hope she's learned her lesson!"

The next day, they saw Penelope on the grounds. She was swallowing some pills, but quite reluctantly. Moving forward, Charlotte saw that it was labeled: *Madame Eller's Pain Pills*. "Pain pills! Is it really that uncomfortable?" Oliver asked Charlotte.

"Nah," she replied. "I just got her good."

Penelope saw them looking at her, and she quickly slipped the bottle away.

They looked at Sam. He looked almost too weak to be walking. His chest was wrapped heavily in bandages. He was whimpering as he took his pills, which were the same as Penelope's.

Finally, Bob had he had bandages on his head that made him look like he was wearing a turban. Everybody sniggered at him as they passed, and he frowned as he took two different types of pills. "*Madame Eller's Headache Cure*," read Ella, "And *Madame Eller's Bone Strengtheners*."

"D'you reckon he cracked his skull?" asked Harry. "Serves him right!"

"Who's Madame Eller?" asked Charlotte.

Harry gaped at her. "Really, Charlotte?"

"What, I just wondered!" Charlotte said hastily. "If it's anything dark or offensive, then just don't say!"

"How come you don't know?" asked Selena. "You were supposed to be the smartest!"

"Selena, I just remembered, she was raised in a non-magical community," said Ella, picking up her book.

"Oh."

"Madame Eller was this talented witch who had a gift for making medicine and mixing antidotes," explained Harry. "She lived like a hundred years ago, and her medicine is still really advanced. Yeah, so, she's practically called a medicinal wonder."

"Didn't know that, Lexington? Didn't you take a glimpse of *Famous Magical Names*? It is practically a classic. What do you even do in the library?" Penelope smirked.

"Go away," muttered Ella. "We're bored of you, you're no threat."

"Don't make me raise my wand on you!" shouted Harry, jumping up.

"No, Harry!" Charlotte yelled, grabbing his sleeve. "No unauthorized dueling is permitted!" She stopped abruptly. Apparently, Penelope did dare raise her wand, and Harry was blasted off his feet. Several girls screamed.

"No!" shouted Selena.

"Fire!" Harry shouted the first spell that came into his mind and pointed his wand carelessly. He set two maple trees on fire, and more people ran and screamed. Some people hid behind trees and bushes until the fire spread, and almost every bit of greenery was alight. Smoke rose high and thick, and people began to panic.

"Hold it!" shouted a voice. "Prefect coming through! No panicking, stay clear of trees and bushes!"

"Kat!" he then shrieked. "Katherine!" And one second later, hurried footsteps sounded. Locating anything and anyone through the smoke was impossible. Charlotte's eyes watered, and she coughed. She remembered what she'd learned in fire drills in her non-magical school, and she stayed close to the ground. "Alert the teachers!" unmistakably, it was Herald. "I can't keep the fire in check for long!"

Katherine ran inside the school, and Herald shouted, "Water!" It had almost no effect. The fire flickered and momentarily subsided. Then, it rose up and roared, bigger and more ferocious than before. The smoke cleared slightly, however, and Charlotte began gasping for breath.

Suddenly, a loud, clear voice shouted, "Water!" And Charlotte actually felt some drops of water on her arms. A squeaky voice soon followed suit, and more water droplets rained down on Charlotte. The smoke cleared immensely. Charlotte looked around, coughing. Harry sat beside her, looking horrified. She sighed and quickly turned away.

Next, a stern female voice shouted, "Water!" like the others, and then did the fire extinguish by bits.

Next, a child's voice sounded. Charlotte assumed it was a Prefect's.

The smoke cleared entirely. Charlotte panted, wheezing for breath. After her lungs cleared, she looked around. There was Herald looking pale but determined, Professor Watonburn surprised and slightly anguished, Professor Historic concentrating on distinguishing the fire, and Professor Austin, looking absolutely furious. Charlotte looked at Harry. He was staring at Professor Watonburn, eyes wide with shock and horror. He was biting his lip, pale as a ghost. Finally, with a last blast of water, the flames went out.

The grounds looked horrible. All the bushes and trees were black and withered, the grass on the floor dead and roasted. Ash coated the floor, and small bits of embers were still crackling.

Professor Watonburn let out another jet of water and washed everyone over, and put out the smallest of embers. Suddenly, he looked furious. "Change robes," he said in a harsher tone than usual, "and gather in the auditorium in fifteen minutes." He whipped around and returned briskly to the school

"Oh, no!" moaned Harry. Penelope gave Harry a satisfied smirk and walked away also.

"Come on, Harry," Charlotte said. "It'll be fine, and we'll be there with you!" She dragged him to his feet and led him towards the school. Once they were in the entrance hall, they split up. Harry and Charlotte went to the top-tier common room, and Selena, Ella, and Oliver headed to the second-tier common room.

"I feel so bad for Harry!" moaned Ella. "But he shouldn't have lost control!"

"We all feel the same way," Selena assured her. "For now, let's just pull on some dry robes and get to the auditorium."

They met back in the entrance hall ten minutes later. "Come on now," whispered Charlotte pacifyingly.

They accompanied Harry to the auditorium, where they sat in the last row.

After another five minutes, the auditorium was full, and all attention was given to the stage. Professor Watonburn emerged from behind the stage curtains. Harry tensed.

"I would like the culprit to confess," he said in an angry tone. "Please, do not lie; I can tell."

Harry drew a deep breath and stood up. All the heads in the auditorium turned to look at him. He ignored them and took another deep breath, then walked down the aisle. Professor Watonburn was staring at him with an expression Charlotte couldn't read.

The expression was surprised, approving, and angry all at the same time. His eyebrows were furrowed with anger. He was nodding very politely, yet his eyes were curved into a curious expression.

Harry ambled down the aisle slowly. Charlotte was biting her lip so hard that tiny drops of blood formed on her lips, and she was squeezing her hands together so tightly that her knuckles were turning a pearly white.

Finally, Harry reached the stage. He clambered on and stood in front of Professor Watonburn. He surveyed him.

"You were involved in the burning of school property," he said, "and it was a very dreadful event, yes?" He looked at Harry. "But!"

Harry looked up hopefully.

"But, you showed great honesty and courage in confessing that must be rewarded. It takes bravery, but also a sense of righteous morale to do this."

Charlotte released her hands and sighed with relief.

Professor Watonburn continued, "But, all the same, there must be a punishment." Charlotte began to become tense again. "But, I have not had enough time to think about the correct punishment," said Professor Watonburn, "and when I do find one that suits, I'll send you a message to come to my study. You may be dismissed." Professor Watonburn straightened up and nodded curtly at Harry.

Harry ran off stage and quickly resumed his seat beside Charlotte.

Professor Watonburn now was addressing the entire school. "Please, let me warn you that the next time that any damage to school property will be punished very severely. Dismissed!"

Everyone began to rise. Harry sighed long and loud. "Come on. The worst hasn't come yet. In fact, I almost wish Professor Watonburn told the punishment. I'm getting, I don't know, jumpy."

"I'm glad you're trying to encourage yourself," Selena said and smiled at Harry.

TEN

Trouble

The following week passed without incident. Harry was downcast and pensive the whole time and very irritable. The five of them all gave the dirtiest looks they could muster to Penelope whenever they crossed paths. Other than that, the week was very normal.

On a Wednesday, the five of them were exiting the dining hall after lunch, discussing possible activities for the next fifteen minutes, in which they were free. Harry had been completely silent for the last two days.

"You should get your History of Magic homework done," Charlotte was scolding Oliver. "You've got a few inches left, just do it!"

"I told you, I'm having writing block," Oliver retorted.

"You know full well that Professor Historic will not accept that," said Charlotte. "You know his temper."

"Oh, hey!" Penelope had arrived on the scene. Ella groaned audibly.

Today, Penelope had a silver butterfly clip in her hair. Selena was first to spot it. Her eyes narrowed as her hand subconsciously traveled to her head, where a similar clip was nestled in her shiny locks.

"Harry, I heard you got detention! I'm not joking, I was sent to deliver this to you!" Penelope held out a detention slip scathingly. "From the shouting-in-the-library incident. And Selena, come look, you too!"

She gave Selena the slip, which seemed to bulge slightly. Penelope left with a smirk.

"This is going to be terrible!" groaned Harry, speaking for the first time in days, as he opened the envelope. "Why couldn't I have given it a little thought?"

"It's...fine, Harry! It was just a few words in the library! It was a little accident," said Ella.

"A little accident?" bellowed Harry, suddenly turning fierce. "What channel are you on? I'm talking about the fire thing! Do you think I care whether or not I get detention for shouting in the library? I know it was Penelope, nobody cares!"

It was evident Harry was still blaming himself for the fire on the grounds.

"No! I...I...just meant that—well, Professor Watonburn could fix the grounds with a swish of his wand!" stammered Ella, very taken aback. "Besides, we're on a magical stretch of land, it's summer all-year-round, is it not?"

Charlotte stepped in. "Actually, it *was*. But then, a group of students voiced their collective disappointment because winter was their favorite season, and they asked the headmaster at the time to enchant the seasons so that they functioned normally so that they could spend time in the snow and do their favorite winter—"

"Alright, miss smarty-pants! But, Ella, what are you thinking?" bellowed Harry. "Apologizing doesn't cut it, I nearly killed us!"

"I...I didn't...mean it that way!" wailed Ella. "I only...only...wanted to say that...stop blaming yourself!"

Sam and Bob walked past, but Penelope was suspiciously not among them.

"Really? It's not that easy!" Harry shouted.

"Mister Snow, how *dare* you make such a racket in the Entrance Hall considering the situations you're already in this last week!"

Professor Katz of the Divination department came storming in. She dropped her papers on a nearby bench and walked towards Harry.

"Detention! Tomorrow afternoon!"

Professor Eloise reached into a shoulder-strap purse and took out a piece of parchment and a quill. She scribbled something on it before handing it to Harry. "Detention slip," she said simply. She turned around and flicked her wand as she passed the scattered papers. She pointed her wand at the papers, and they all arranged themselves in mid-air and flew into her hands.

Harry frowned after her. He turned around. "GOODBYE!" he roared at Ella and stormed away.

Selena grimaced after him.

"It's all my fault!" whispered Ella. "I upset him."

"No, it's not your fault!" shouted Selena firmly, but with a strange edge to her voice. "You tried to comfort him, and he took his anger on you for a terrible reason! It's actually...*un*reasonable! Completely unreasonable! That means with *no* reason!"

"Yeah, we know that, Selena!" said Charlotte.

Selena glared after Harry, who was walking into the dining hall.

"Let's try and talk to him, what do you think?" Charlotte suggested.

"Yeah," said Oliver. "Come, Ella."

"No!" shouted Ella, bursting into tears, and she ran away as well, up the stairs and out of sight.

"We've got to go get her!" said Charlotte. "Come on!"

She brushed her hair out of her face and ran.

They went up the same set of stairs Ella did, but they did not find her at the top.

"Where's Selena?"

They'd suddenly realized Selena was no longer with them. As they were turning to go back, Selena appeared at the top of the steps.

"Sorry! But I think we're late; we won't be able to find Ella!"

"No, we're not!" Charlotte panted. "Hurry!" She sprinted up more steps, Selena and Oliver trailing after her. "Quick, come on!" she shouted when she reached the top. She looked around. She caught a glimpse of a blue bag embroidered with pink flowers turning the corner. Having seen this bookbag many times before, she knew it was Ella's.

"Here, this way!" said Charlotte, and she ran through the crowd to where the bag was a minute ago. When she reached the spot, she turned the way the bag went and continued to sprint. However, they soon reached a dead end.

Selena and Oliver caught up.

"I'm sure she went this way!" panted Charlotte.

"She must have gone into the common room," said Selena. Selena looked at Charlotte's puzzled look.

"The Second-tiers' common room," she added. She drew her wand and tapped an old brick.

"Violet flowers!" she yelled the newest password. The brick popped out to reveal a hole. "Selena Emma Caroline," she said, and the hole became bigger. "Wait here," she said to the other two and shoved aside the tapestry concealing the room. As she walked through, the hole began to decrease in size. Almost instinctively, Charlotte stuck out a hand to stop it, but then, a ghost appeared.

He was pearly white and almost transparent. He had a sullen face and an old-fashioned robe embedded with gems, and atop his head was a French hat with a protruding peacock feather. He gazed at the horrified Charlotte glumly.

"*Of all the years I've been installed,*
I am here, held enthralled.
I created much terror among the peeps,
For my spirit was evil, indeed.
To keep me in check, the ones of wisdom,
Chained me, forbade me, to leave with a spell.
So I am here to guard this "clubhouse,"
But I can be free when one touches the frame, like now.
And if they want to imprison me again,
They'll have to find me and force me in.
Thank you, I say, from my view,
But will the magic world forgive you too?
Oh, I do not know, the way these new minds think,
But be careful, you little thing.
All my life was once misery,
Hoping someone will come and free me.
But now my deepest wish has come true,
And it's all because of you, yes you!

Tried so hard but is just a fry,
Never met one who has that right.
And now I live, as happy as a god,
For you saved me, oh, what a thought!
And now I leave and say goodbye.
Until we meet, away I'll fly.
Goodbye, and thank you, for what you did,
You have freed one who committed a sin."

He nodded at Charlotte, dove into the wall, and vanished.

"Oh, no!" whispered Charlotte, staring at the place he had vanished. "Today is the worst!"

Oliver shrugged. "I don't know, really. Once—"

Charlotte turned around and faced him. "Think about it! Harry still blames himself for setting the entire grounds on fire, and he'll have to face a horrible punishment soon, and he abandoned us. Then, Ella ran away because she was sad, and now we've lost her as well. And then, by accident, I let the ghost of some lunatic tyrant out and he's going to cause trouble, and *I'll* be in trouble! I can't wait to see what comes next!" She grabbed her bag and ran down the steps.

"Okay, so this *is* the worst day ever!" muttered Oliver.

"It's all right, Ella. We'll fix you up," came Selena's soft voice, "and what's happened with you?" she asked Oliver.

He explained to them every last detail that he could remember. "... and then Charlotte just turned and ran?" asked Selena.

"Yeah, right!" said Oliver impatiently.

"Mind, I'm going to Professor Watonburn!" Selena said and pushed Ella away from her. She rushed down the steps, stomping her foot. Ella sobbed again, and before Oliver could do anything, she turned back into the common room.

"Geez! What in the world?" she heard Oliver yell.

Hee, hee, rustle, rustle, rustle.

Ella's brain took a while processing it. "Hee, hee?" she muttered.

It was undoubtedly a human creating these noises. She immediately whipped around and darted out of the common room. There, she looked around. An emerald green bag embroidered with silk patterns lay on the floor. She picked it up and opened it. She stared at the name tag: *Selena Emma Caroline.*

"This isn't Selena's writing!" she said and groped into the bag. The first thing that she touched was a heavy leather book. She read the title. "*Potions of the Worst!*" she read. She flipped to the first page and read. "*Morphing Potion is a potion to make one take the appearance of another person, an animal, or an object.*" She skipped the recipe and looked at the bottom of the chapter. "*It must look colorless, like water at first. Then, you must add an object representative of the person, animal, or thing you wish to represent. For example, you may add the treasured possession of a person, the fur of a dog, or a needle from a cactus. The potion will soon take the color of the object you inserted. Then, you drink. The closer the object you added is to the thing you wish to impersonate is, the more accurate the results will be.*"

Ella reread the chapter. It didn't seem like anything Selena would read. It didn't even feel like something Charlotte would read. It felt dark and evil.

Even so, she examined the page again. This time careful not to overlook anything. But she didn't find any notes or doodles or anything peculiar at all. She ran her hand up and down the page and found the upper left corner was folded back into a tiny dog-ear.

Ella set down the book and reached into the bag once more. Next, she felt a vial. She drew it out and found a few wood shavings. It took Ella a moment to understand this, then she remembered Selena telling her of a few unknown scratches on her wand. Finally, she felt a corked bottle. It contained a liquid that looked almost exactly like water. She eyed it. It was obvious someone was trying to take the form of Selena, and now, she was doing something with Professor Watonburn!

"No, I mustn't run to Professor Watonburn. Besides this, there isn't much proof!" But her heart was pumping. What if it was true that someone was an impostor? What if she didn't run to Professor Watonburn? How might that affect her? Mountain View? The world?

Ella's eyes widened with fear. She threw all three things in her own bag and ran. She hoped that whoever was taking Selena's form would not know the way to Professor Watonburn's office.

Squinting to keep out the wind from her eyes, she dashed down from her dorm and ran towards the high tower. She heard footsteps seemingly going the same way as her, and getting closer. She closed her eyes and strained her muscles. Finally, she caught a glimpse of a lock of shiny, black, wavy hair winding through the crowd.

She ran with all her might, and when she reached the top of the tower, she saw the Selena impostor already slipping into Professor Watonburn's office.

Ella didn't know how they found out how to get in, but at the moment, Ella didn't care. She ran across the corridor and into Professor Watonburn's conference room. She saw the supposedly fake Selena shouting, "Ram horns!" to the portrait of Mountain View, then step inside.

The tapestry magically returned to the wall.

"R-ram h-horns!" Ella, in-turn, panted at the painting. It fell, and she dashed inside.

Selena was standing in front of Professor Watonburn's desk. Professor Watonburn and Selena both whirled around when they heard Ella's footsteps.

"P-professor!" panted Ella. "I need to talk, in private! *She* can't be here!" she indicated Selena.

Professor Watonburn eyed her. "Please, that's very impolite," he said. "But if it is urgent, just please remember your manners next time."

He led Selena out the door. "Change the password to get in, Professor!" pleaded Ella.

"Sure," he replied simply. "Sour apple spray!" He muttered while flicking his wand.

Eventually, he looked at the back of the portrait carefully and returned to his seat, smiling. "I know, I know. Weird choice, but it just came into my head!" He adjusted his position. "Yes, what would you like to say?"

"Morphing Potion!" shouted Ella. "Someone, perhaps Penelope Brown, is, well, taking the form of my friend Selena Caroline!" she said.

"Oh, dear me, Ella. Yet you see, I can't do anything without proof!"

Professor Watonburn shook his head. "And that's a very serious accusation."

"I have proof!" said Ella. She reached into her bag.

"This is not Selena's handwriting!" cried Ella. She pointed at the name tag. "*This* is!"

She had just found a crumpled piece of paper stuffed in the bottom of the bag. It was supposed to be her last Charms essay.

Professor Watonburn took the parchment and the bag. He stared at them with great concentration.

Eventually, he looked up. "You say that someone, perhaps Miss Penelope Brown is taking the form of Selena?" he asked.

"Yes, correct!" shouted Ella.

"But, as you see, this evidence is not strong! Perhaps it is just Selena asking another student to help her write her name, or her mother did it. Parents do these kind of things!" He smiled.

"And these!" shouted Ella, withdrawing each of the three things. "Why on earth would Selena want a book on potions?" she asked. "Especially this one!" She opened the book and pointed to the first page, whose edge was dog-eared.

"Isn't this Morphing Potion?" she asked and brought out the vial of watery liquid. "And Selena once told me about scratches on her wand, and look!" she took out the bottle corking several curly wood shavings

"This is–yes, way more convincing," said Professor Watonburn. He examined each of the objects again, this time more carefully. Finally, he sighed, long and deep. "Then, where is the real Selena Caroline?" he asked.

"I have no idea," shrugged Ella.

"Then who do you think might be taking the form of Selena, Ella?" Professor Watonburn asked.

"Penelope!" said Ella.

"Proof?" prompted Professor Watonburn.

Ella thought hard. Suddenly, an image of a dusty book being set down on the table in front of her flashed through her mind. Recalling her memories, Ella remembered the day Penelope took a book from the Restricted Section and commented about Professor Stoddart in front of them in the library before Harry and Selena had shouted at her. *Potions and Poisons*, a restricted book. "I remember! I saw her borrowing books from the restricted section on poisons and potions! And of course, she's already a suspect working against us and the closing the dungeon!" She grinned.

"So, you're telling me that you suspect Miss Penelope Brown gave your friend Selena Caroline a dose of the Sleeping Potion, and she fell asleep somewhere?" he asked.

"Yes!" Ella said.

"But how do you think Penelope gave Selena this potion? It would be quite ridiculous to suspect that Penelope just walked up to her in the corridors! Besides, the Sleeping Potion is a horribly hard brew. I, myself had trouble with it in my second year, how do you think a first-year could whip it up well?" he smiled.

"Well, she was always the best at potions in the year, besides Charlotte. She's even been boasting that she could pretty much do anything, and that she was like royalty, and it was required in her family, blah blah blah. She said she had private tutors, and that's why she's so smart or whatever. She could've slipped it into her drink!" said Ella.

Professor Watonburn sighed again. "Time to be forceful to get the truth. Please, bring Selena to me," he said.

"Well, isn't Selena actually Penelope?" Ella asked.

"Maybe. Bring her in. We'll invite her in for a cup of tea and congratulate her in her potions scores."

Ella reached for the tapestry and pulled it down. Selena was pacing rather sullenly there.

"Selena, come in!" Ella said. "I told Professor Watonburn about your potions quiz! He says he'd love to congratulate you!" The fake Selena sighed, looking quite relieved, though a little suspicious. She followed Ella into the room, and Professor Watonburn pretended to be jolly as well. "May I offer you a cup of tea?" he finally asked.

"Ooh, yes!" she grinned as she entered.

Professor Watonburn poured tea for each of them, handed a cup to Ella, and one to Penelope. He took a sip.

Penelope accepted her cup and followed Professor Watonburn's example. She took a small sip, and in the moment her eyes were lowered, Professor Watonburn drew his wand, quick as lightning, and cast a truth charm on her.

For a moment, it seemed as if she knew what was happening and what she did wrong, but it was too late now. Her eyes rolled to face Professor Watonburn, and with a faint *pop*, they were suddenly fixed and rigid.

Then, her face began to morph. It was strange, each part of her body was altered one by one. It was both amazing and horrifying, and very soon, she became a totally different person. Ella leaned forward expectantly, and indeed, it turned out to be Penelope.

Professor Watonburn set down his cup. "Have you had any Morphing Potion?" he asked.

"Yes," she replied, expressionless.

"Tell me, then, everything that has to do with it."

He sat back down and took a sip of tea.

"Auntie Corps and Auntie Vodvanov were the only children of Dylan Ablitan and Maris Copette. When Auntie Corps was thirteen, and Auntie Vodvanov was ten, their parents divorced, so Grandmother Maris was left with the two children."

"Wow we're in for a whole Penelope Brown family history session," Ella sniggered to herself.

"She later married another man, Grandfather Copette. She had my mother with him. Grandmother Maris and Grandfather Copette were secret supporters of Dark Magic. When mother turned old enough, as she was a decade or so younger than my aunties, Grandmother Maris and Grandfather Copette decided to try something else. They sent her to the all-girls Tukain Institute of Magic, which has in recent years, been closed due to the inter-student dueling death toll.

"As this school felt closer to dark magic, mother instantly became Grandmother Maris and Grandfather Copette's favorite.

"Thus, they thought mother was the special one, and she passed the bloodline and gifts of dark magic to me, so I became their favorite grandchild.

"As for my new prominent place in the family, I was told things Sam and Bob would never get to hear. They revealed to me everything they could say about the Dungeon of Unknown Doom. They said it had been opened, and the destined destroyer was at none other than Waterside School of Magic. Due to my importance in the family, I was expected to find out who it was.

"It was too obvious. Historic, who has never been patient with any student that passed through his class, talked to Charlotte in such a warm, paternal fashion. There was so much favoritism, even by the first day. Two teachers walked Charlotte personally to her next classes.

"I wrote to Grandmother Maris and Grandfather Copette immediately. They were absolutely delighted. Now, I needed to spy on Ella Ross and her friends. So, one day, when that Selena Caroline wasn't watching, I slipped some Sleeping Potion into her drink, and she fell asleep. I hid her in a cupboard and checked on her every hour.

"I took her bag and found she hadn't written her name on it yet. I was afraid something was wrong, like it wasn't hers, and the others would mention it. I just, had a feeling, so I signed it for her. During the weekdays, I was Penelope; during the weekends, I was Selena. I told everyone except Sam and Bob that mother was ill, and I had to go see her every weekend," she stopped.

As she explained, Professor Watonburn looked very deep in thought. "Oh goodness," he would mutter occasionally.

Suddenly, Ella thought of something.

"How'd you give Selena the potion today? I saw you just before we—I, um, ran away. And what'd you mean when you said our privacy would be gone? Also, what about those rustling sounds I've heard?" she asked.

Professor Watonburn looked up curiously. The fake Selena, who was now actually Penelope, continued without any expression. "When I gave Selena her detention slip from Professor Boock, I slipped in a piece of candy; I also wrote a little note impersonating someone else, saying that she had a secret admirer. I had soaked it in Sleeping Draught, she put it in her mouth immediately and feel asleep just as you guys were running after Ella. I couldn't believe my luck, the corridors were empty! I stashed her away and drank the Morphing Potion, and came after you. And of course, I was pretending to be Selena. It would look very suspicious if I didn't know how to get into the common room or Watonburn's office, so our family sent a fellow friend and supporter of the dark arts to spy on you, and it looks as if he hasn't done a very good job of being quiet."

"Then why haven't my friends heard her?"

"That I cannot say for sure," replied Penelope. "Perhaps you're cursed? Have you wandered into the Dungeon at any point?"

While Ella was considering it, for she had no idea where the dungeon was, and she thought it fully possible she could've accidentally wandered in at some point, suddenly Penelope's eyeballs began to move. Her face softened and was no longer expressionless. She blinked.

"Oh, no!" she cried. "What've I done? Mother and father, Grandmother Maris and Grandfather Copette, Auntie Corps and Auntie Vodvanov will kill me!"

"Professor Watonburn?" Ella whispered.

"Yes, Ella?" he asked.

"Can you *please* do that truth charm again? There's something else I want to ask."

"No," he replied. "We've had enough for today."

He looked at Penelope. "So, you *are* plotting against Ella. Oh, dear. Tell me, no—look at me in the eye—has your family secretly supported Dagina?"

"Y-yes...Professor!" choked Penelope. "And...well...never mind. Now I'm going to be disinherited!"

"Never mind what?" Professor Watonburn asked.

"Oh, what's the point? Dagina...she...she...she will rise again! She's just lying low at the moment!"

"Oh, dear," Professor Watonburn said. "I suspected as much. Penelope, thank you for the honesty. Worry not, I am already organizing a response team. I have seen the signs. But first, better alert Duncan."

He closed his eyes and began spinning on the spot. Ella watched in amazement. He spun faster and faster like a top, until he was a blur of blue and white. With a flash, he disappeared. Ella screamed.

"Where did he go?" she asked Penelope frantically.

"He only materialized elsewhere," Penelope assured her. "He'll be back."

A few minutes later, with another flash of light, Professor Watonburn reappeared exactly where he had gone.

"Oh dear, was Duncan happy!" he said. "He's an intern journalist, and as he's my friend, I've been trying to help him score a top article."

Professor Watonburn stood in front of Penelope. "Dear girl, you are truly very sharp and attentive. I cannot have expected any more of a student. I also do understand the gravity of all that has happened today," he muttered, "but I can hardly let you go back to your own family. It will not yield pleasant outcomes."

"Yeah!" she shouted.

"Oh, I know this is going to be hard on you, but I think you're best off living with another wizarding family, Penelope? How about Charlotte Lexington's family? One day she told me how lonely she was at home without siblings."

Penelope looked up. "Y-yes! I'll go!"

Ella's eyes widened.

"Sorry, Ella," Penelope muttered at her.

"I'll write to Charlotte's uncle and your parents. Both of you are now excused," Professor Watonburn said, standing up. "And make sure to tell Charlotte, Harry, Oliver, and Selena the new password's 'Sour Apple Spray'," he whispered to Ella.

"Sir," Ella couldn't help but say it, "you hear the worst witch is going to rise, and your first thought is to help your friend?"

Professor Watonburn smiled. "You have no idea of the power of public realization and friendship. One day, you'll understand no one can singly fight a group. No matter what group it is."

Ella nodded and turned away.

As they slowly went away from the door, Ella couldn't help continuously sneaking glances at Penelope. "Penelope, is that you?" she finally asked. "You seriously said 'sorry Ella?'"

"Yes, I am sorry!" shouted Penelope, bursting into confessions. "I was just jealous!" she sniffed. "My whole life, I had to live up to everyone else's expectations and standards. I tried being mean and gruff when I got here but it's not in my nature. I wanted nothing more than to be enough for my family, and I didn't enjoy it. Everyday, reflecting on my words, on my choices, my actions. I could never be myself, I could never be free. I'm so sorry for all the harm I caused to you and to the whole wizarding world, because in truth, I did cause a lot. I sent a lot of things and information to my family that I wish I could take back. I want to help you Ella, I really do!"

"Aw," Ella said, putting an arm around Penelope. "It's alright... there, there. I forgive you, we all do. Thank you for telling me this, really."

"Thanks, Ella," she smiled. "Honestly, you make me feel better... I've got to make up for the damage I made somehow though."

Ella shrugged.

Penelope's face suddenly darkened. "My grandfather will whip me to bits the next time I see him."

"Then, don't see him!" suggested Ella. "Go live with Charlotte and her uncle! They won't have such a grudge against you."

"Won't they, though?" Penelope asked. "I mean, will they forgive as easily as you did?"

"I'm sure we will be able to talk some sense into them," Ella said reassuringly. "By the way, where *is* the real Selena?" she asked.

"I pushed her into the broom cupboard," answered Penelope, blushing. "It was the nearest secluded place I could find at the time. She should be stirring by now. I could go find Charlotte and Harry in our common room, and you find Oliver and get Selena. We'll round 'em up, and then we can explain."

"Sounds good," said Ella.

They walked a few minutes in silence, and then Penelope laughed. "You won't believe it, but I had to share a dorm with Charlotte! Arguments every night!" She made a funny face.

They both chortled.

ELEVEN

Bit by Bit

They parted when they reached the ground floor. Penelope went upstairs to find Charlotte and Harry. Ella went to the secluded little broom cupboard on the first floor and found Selena stirring. After some vigorous shaking on Ella's part, Selena woke up.

"Why do I keep waking up in dark, secluded places?" she asked groggily.

"Later," Ella replied, and told her to wait in the entrance hall.

Ella dashed up the steps and into the common room. To make things easier, thankfully, Oliver wasn't in the boys' dorms. He was working near the common room fireplace. She grabbed him and told him there was an emergency and she didn't have enough time to explain, then dragged him into the entrance hall.

Penelope was back, firmly binding Charlotte and Harry.

"Penelope, listen here!" Charlotte was muttering. "Because we're in school, and we're classmates, I am not going to harm you, but if you start it—!"

"Relax!" Ella said, laughing, and together, they explained the entire plan. Ella had persuaded Charlotte with elaborate details of Penelope's story, which Charlotte cross-examined expertly, like a lawyer. In the end, both she and Selena were all for it. Harry and Oliver basically just said it was rather odd, and they wouldn't hesitate to keep an eye on her.

"Come on, you two!" shouted Ella. "We used *a Truth Charm*! You should see the effects of it! Penelope's eyeballs just froze, and she talked without expression! Basically, she was droning on and on without stopping or anything!"

"Exactly," intervened Charlotte.

"Okay, fine, we get it!" said Harry.

They stared at each other in silence for a moment. Oliver and Harry exchanged nervous looks. Finally, they seemed to have reached a telepathic agreement and caved in.

"Welcome to the gang, I guess," Oliver told Penelope.

"Yep," Harry said. "Welcome. But you better not do anything funny on our watch. We'll trust you but... " Harry and Oliver looked at each other again. "One false move and we'll jinx you so bad you'll be paralyzed for the rest of your life."

Penelope laughed semi-nervously. "Yes sir," she mocked.

Charlotte felt it was time to get down to business. "Now that we've got Penelope, we've got to pay more attention to the Dungeon of Unknown Doom!" she said. "Penelope's got *almost* all the information we need, so for once and for all, let's just get this over with."

They told her to put her idea on hold for a bit since almost a quarter of the semester was nearly over and the time here to start worrying about their final exams.

According to their teachers, the transition and introduction time was over, and the real work was about to begin.

One week later, they were working on their latest Potions homework in the library. "I just *wish* you would all put this stuff out of your minds!" Charlotte whispered.

"I never thought I'd see the day when you wouldn't take school and homework seriously, Charlotte!" hissed Selena.

"Oh, you two, I can't concentrate!" Penelope complained. "I've just written, *I never thought I'd see the day when you wouldn't take school and homework seriously!* Instead of: *Add your crushed griffin claws to the potion and stir for five minutes!*"

Ella stifled a small giggle. Penelope smiled herself and took out her wand to erase the ink. Sam and Bob stalked by. They cast confused looks at Penelope but didn't utter a word. Ella wasn't even sure if they knew how to talk. After all, they hardly ever said anything.

Penelope turned around to fetch more ink out of her bag. Her glance swept over them. Sam and Bob tried to hide behind a nearby shelf, but their plump figures were simply too large to have been concealed. Penelope stood up and shot warning looks at them. They quickly shuffled out from behind the shelf and started away. They glanced back. Penelope shook her head and beckoned them towards her, so they looked at each other and shuffled towards her.

"Leave us *alone*," she hissed warningly when they were close enough. "Send a pigeon to Grandfather if you want, I don't care! Just leave. Never find me again. Never speak to me." She glared at them and shooed them away.

"Nice," snickered Harry.

Finally, the weekend arrived. Ella was planning to sleep in late and have a great big breakfast afterward, then spend the day exploring the mountains and their mysteries, which she was obsessed with.

"*Get up!*" hissed somebody as they shook her hard.

"What? Huh?" she asked, rolling around. She checked her alarm clock. It was ten minutes to five o'clock.

She glanced up. Selena was standing there, puffy-eyed as well. "What's the matter?" asked Ella, sitting up.

"Charlotte wants us up nice and early so we can sort through our studying and get to work on the Dungeon," Selena replied.

Ella rubbed her eyes and grabbed her bag halfheartedly. "At this ungodly hour?"

Selena scoffed. "You know Charlotte, her whole obsession with learning is ungodly."

Ella gave a halfhearted chuckle as she threw back her covers.

"Meet you downstairs," said Selena, and she walked out of the room.

Ella cast envious glances at Chloe and Amy's lumpy forms under their blankets and started down the staircase. Selena was waiting near the entrance of the common room. The fire in the fireplace was out, and loud snoring came from upstairs frequently. A few early birds circled in the sky outside. The sun was slowly ascending, sending soft pink rays to fill the horizon, dying the pure white clouds ombre from gold to scarlet.

Ella yawned and followed Selena out of the common room. Oliver, also yawning, stood behind an agitated Harry, whose eyebrows were furrowed. Penelope slumped against the wall, trying to get a few moments of extra sleep. Charlotte stood smilingly in front of them, the only enthusiastic member of their team, and upon seeing Ella, she said, "This is going to be our new routine for the weekends, Okay?"

Charlotte smiled innocently and began descending the stairs. Ella was so sleepy she almost tripped on the last couple of steps.

Charlotte led them into the dining hall. No students were up, and neither were any teachers.

The procession of six made their way into the hall, and as they sat down, utensils and a generous meal suddenly appeared. They hurried and gulped down some oatmeal and toast, and at precisely five minutes after five, Charlotte led them all and flung them out of the doors and into the grounds.

As the crisp and cold morning breeze wafted across them all, Ella began to feel alive. She blinked and felt wide-awake now. She raised her hands and rubbed them against her arms, a little chilly in the cold dawn.

As Charlotte led them back in and towards the library, she explained, "I obviously thought we weren't going to get our work done properly with all of you dozing off all the time. I had to refresh you like that."

They all worked in the library until seven. That's when faint footsteps indicated the first students, and possibly teachers, heading down for breakfast. The refreshing aftermaths of the cold breeze were wearing off, so Charlotte went and opened all the windows in the library until they were so cold their teeth were chattering, and then they asked Charlotte to close most of them.

At seven-thirty, most of the students jumbled in. Slowly, a sharp the noise level started rising, and things got chatty and loud. They looked around, but Professor Boock wasn't there.

"Where is Professor Boock?" asked Ella in an undertone.

"I don't know," responded Charlotte. "Let's work somewhere else, maybe?"

As they were packing—*BANG! BANG! BANG!*

"What rascals!"

Professor Boock returned from giving Mr. Bromhead her morning book status report, which contained information about which books had been borrowed, which had been destroyed, which had been damaged, and such.

Two second-tier boys, one lanky and thin, the other short and stout, were chased out of the library by Professor Boock. Their heights made a considerate contrast as they bolted between the tables and out the door.

"After I'd just reported to Mr. Bromhead that two books were in need of magical repairs because of you two!"

They all stifled their laughs and quickly went out on the grounds. The sun was up high now, and it was warm. They sat on benches, basking in the warm light.

"Oh, no! Not David!" Oliver suddenly yelled and flung his books over his head.

"Who?" Charlotte asked.

"David, my stepbrother!" replied Oliver, scrambling to hide himself.

"Which one is he?" Charlotte asked, scanning all the students currently out on the grounds.

"The one walking towards us!" Oliver replied as he slid off his seat.

"You didn't tell us that you had a brother!" said Selena.

"I said, *step*brother!"

He ducked behind Harry way too late.

David was a tall boy that simply towered over them, with curly brown hair eyes. His eyes were mildly reminiscent of Oliver's, but they were narrowed maliciously on this occasion. He glared at Oliver.

"Heard your friend set the grounds on fire," his eyes flickered towards Harry.

"Okay, that was a while ago," Harry muttered. "And I've already been punished enough."

"Well, guess what, Oliver?" David continued menacingly. "I've been made a Prefect, and I'm giving him detention!"

He smirked and brought out a piece of parchment. *"Detention slip for first-year, Top-tier, H. Snow. Eighteen o'clock sharp in the Dungeons. Help Professor Stoddart as he rearranges Potion ingredients. Signed, Prefect David—"*

"Flame!" Selena directed her wand at him, and the paper burst into flames. David dropped it in alarm.

After it sizzled and coiled into ashes, Ella shouted, *"Water!"* and water burst from her wand and extinguished the small fire. David looked shocked. Then, he squared his shoulders and turned away.

After that, they worked until eleven-thirty, when the lunch bell rang.

They hurried to the dining hall and gobbled up their lunch. They took a rest outside and went back to work at one o'clock. They worked until five, and that's when Charlotte shouted, "Done!" She had completed her charms essay and pulled out her Dark Arts book.

"Could you *please* help us?" groaned Harry.

Charlotte frowned. "I have told you, you are learning for yourself. If you copy down everything *I* write, then you wouldn't learn anything!"

"We'll read it through thoroughly!" said Oliver. "We'll remember, we'll paraphrase it!"

"Never again!" Charlotte sighed, pulling out her essay. Harry took it and copied down everything, word for word.

Oliver and Penelope shared it, and then Ella and Selena looked it through. Though the different tiers had separate curriculums, the content they studied was similar.

Once everyone's homework was well finished, Charlotte took them to the grounds and started to discuss the Dungeon.

"Okay," said Charlotte. "First, we have to divide us into the exploration crew and the land crew."

They nodded, and Charlotte continued.

"First, we need to train our team," she said, taking out five pieces of parchment. "I've been spending most of my free time coming up with the most useful and likely used spells, potions, and skills. Once everybody's mastered these, we can go."

She handed them around. "It's almost dinner time," she concluded. "You guys can look through them as we eat." Then they rushed into the dining hall.

They gobbled up their last meal of the day and went outside to train on the spells. Penelope had a hard time with the Fall Back Jinx; Selena had problems with the deflection charm; Ella spent all night trying to learn the severing charm; Oliver had never even heard of the banishing charm; Harry couldn't figure out how to work the knockout jinx. All in all, the evening was rather disastrous.

They slumped into their beds past midnight. Few of them accomplished anything in terms of learning new spells to use in the Dungeon. Everyone, except Charlotte, hoped that the failure had diminished her hopes, but how incredibly wrong they were.

Their failure only made Charlotte think they weren't working hard enough. The following day, she had them up at four-thirty, and she had them up before five the next morning as well.

"It's Monday!" complained Harry.

"So, what?" Charlotte snapped. "You were perfectly awake both yesterday and the day before that!"

After lessons, they trained until midnight. At the end of the week, you could see the evident progress they'd made.

During the second weekend, Charlotte started urging them to put even more effort into training.

"I'm not a person who waits around and put things off," she told them sternly, "and if we don't destroy that Dungeon before the school year ends, I'm leaving Mountain View forever!" She dramatically snatched up her wand and furiously demonstrated the darkness spell.

"Geez," muttered Harry.

After another three weeks of training, they could duel like professionals.

"I love being able to turn anything I want into a goat!" shouted

Oliver, transforming a nearby rock to prove his point.

"We will tackle the Dungeon next weekend," shouted Charlotte, and happily high-fived everyone.

"Excuse me, I do not want to interrupt the celebrations," came a voice. They turned around. Professor Watonburn stood there, smiling. "Now, I have not forgotten the burning of school property, Harry," he said. Harry's head drooped. "My first foolish thought was not letting you help your friends in destroying the Dungeon. But, of course, that *would be* quite foolish. Charlotte needs her friends."

Harry tensed.

"So, I have given it some thought and found a more suitable punishment. Though it does have some roots in the old idea."

Harry whimpered. He obviously wanted to go.

"So, I am sorry to mess up your wonderful organization, Charlotte, but I think it would be better if all of you went, and I stood as correspondent outside. So, Harry here, could be an extra backup person for me. I have read accounts of various wizards journeying into the dungeon, and I thought, why risk all of you at once? If you are close to your end, a fresh new arrival would be useful, would it not?"

Harry sighed.

"Harry, you have no idea how sorry I am to do this to you," Professor Watonburn explained. "But, a bad deed requires a punishment, so I am sorry but this will—"

"I'll be back up!"

Penelope was standing there, purple-faced and breathing heavily.

Professor Watonburn surveyed her carefully. Once her breathing calmed, he said, "I truly admire your willingness to help friends, Penelope," he said. "But I am afraid you cannot help take over *punishments*. It's for Harry to learn, not you."

"No, Professor, I...I provoked him!" she said.

Professor Watonburn looked at Penelope. "Still, Harry should learn to keep a cool head and think things through first. You did not make him set the grounds on fire, and so, he must take his own responsibility."

Harry looked at Penelope in surprise as she slowly turned away from Professor Watonburn.

"Professor, I don't think that will work," said Charlotte defiantly. You see, we need Harry to help. There are obstacles that I can't take on alone, but I can conquer with my friends."

"Indeed, and you most certain have a very apt batch of companions," Professor Watonburn gestured to everyone else.

"Yes, but," Charlotte continued. "You see, if... if there is one of those situations, say I got through with these four. Then, we meet another obstacle in which we need Harry's assistance. How is Harry to get to us? He most certainly cannot take the former obstacle alone? That just—just would not work, Professor."

Professor Watonburn studied her, something of a smile playing on his lips.

"Fair point, fair point," he nodded. "And I must say, you have quite convinced me. I suppose then, Harry is obliged to go with you. I suppose a detention would have to do, like any other student. To be honest, I would not have gone to such lengths to think of a penalty if not for... if not for the... well, that does not matter. It is good that we have fixed this up."

He finished with a faint smile, but they continued to stare up at him inquisitively.

"If not for what, Professor?" asked Harry.

"Not to worry, not to worry," said Professor Watonburn. "It is nothing, and it does not concern you directly just yet. So, I will stand as like a correspondent outside by myself, is that right?"

"Professor, please don't bother," Charlotte said earnestly. "We'll be alright, and I'm sure there's not much you can help with outside of the Dungeon. We don't know how long we'll be in there, and we... we can manage. Thanks, thanks though."

"If you are quite sure," Professor Watonburn responded courteously, and did not push. "And, I am quite sorry, but there is another problem to be addressed. Next time Charlotte, please check your calendar."

She dug out a booklet from her robes and flipped it open. Her eyes scanned the page for a moment, and then—"It's *Christmas* next week!" she shouted. "Oh, dear!"

"Yes, it is," said Professor Watonburn smiling. "And what would you all prefer, going home or staying in the school?"

Penelope, Oliver, Ella, and Charlotte yelled, "School!" while Selena and Harry shouted, "Home!"

"If I'm going home, I'd never see any of you again!" moaned Penelope. "Oh, grandfather is going to be horrible to me! I'll die the moment I step foot in that house again."

"And if I go home, I'd have to deal with David the Prefect prat!" complained Oliver.

"Siblings," muttered Ella in turn. "I was so happy to be devoid of Ace at last, I'm not returning in a hurry."

"And *I* don't want to put destroying the Dungeon off any longer!" said Charlotte.

"Well, every Christmas, we have a party, and all our neighbors and relatives come!" said Selena, her eyes glittering. "It's so fun, and I wouldn't wanna miss it! I've got a dress picked out and everything. It's salmon pink and it's got glitter around the collar. I'm not letting my prep go to waste!"

"Yeah, and I want my Christmas presents," added Harry.

"First," said Professor Watonburn, stepping in. "Penelope, oh dear me, I forgot to tell you, but you'll be living with Charlotte now. I talked to both your grandfather and Charlotte's uncle, and they mutually agreed. If you want, we can also go through procedure for you to officially become part of Charlotte's family, for Mr. Lexington is willing to take you in as Charlotte's adoptive sister. Your grandfather, on the other hand, expresses zero interest and complete consent to whatever we may plan."

"Sounds like him," muttered Penelope.

"That's wonderful!" exclaimed Charlotte. "You've got to do this, Penelope, I would love to have you as a sister!"

"Well then, Penelope, Charlotte, come see me in my office whenever you have the time, and we'll work it out," replied Professor Watonburn with a kind smile. "Oh, and Harry, all the Christmas presents will be sent by pigeon delivery."

"Oh, then I would certainly go home!" shouted Penelope. "If *home* means Charlotte's house!" Penelope yelled joyfully.

"Oh, if I get the same amount of presents as I do at home, certainly I'll stay!" added Harry.

"And, Selena?" said Professor Watonburn. "I am not asking or trying to get you to change your mind, but we have a dinner party here as well, *and* we have a very delicious feast."

"Ooh!" whispered Selena. She leaned forward and began questioning Professor Watonburn on the musical arrangements, the food, the games, and the attendees.

"Selena," cried Harry exasperatedly.

Selena blushed and withdrew.

"Oh right," said Professor Watonburn. "I will leave it to you all to make your decisions by yourselves, which I'm sure you're capable of! Good day!" He smiled warmly at them and walked away.

"Come on! Let's stay!" shouted Harry, pumping his fists.

"How about taking a vote?" asked Charlotte. "All in favor of staying in the school this Christmas, raise your hand." She raised her hand with Harry, Oliver, Ella, and Selena.

Penelope looked downcast.

"Come on, it'll be fun!" coaxed Selena. "Dinner parties! Games! Friends!"

Penelope stifled an eye roll. "Yes, Selena, I know. I've got no objections."

Charlotte smiled at her and put an arm around her shoulder. Quietly, she breathed into Penelope's ear, "It's not interesting at all during Christmas at my house. We're better off here."

"I'll take your word for it," Penelope said with a grin.

Christmas was approaching thick and fast. Snow came to the enchanted school. Outside was a silvery-white wonderland, except the lake, which was crystal clear, and turned into a seemingly never-ending skating rink (though there were limits to where this magic extended).

Inside was filled with holiday cheer. Strands of holly and pine wound their way through all the fences and gates. In the dining hall, warm, magical snow fell day and night, coating the ground, and ice statues were placed in the corridors. During break time and dinnertime, the ice statues began to sing Christmas carols, and at almost every meal, there was a sing-along.

In the back of the dining hall stood the biggest evergreen Charlotte had ever seen. Tall and massive, probably ten times taller than Charlotte, it was filled with ornaments that sparkled and jingled.

Four days before Christmas Eve, she wrapped up her presents and prepared them.

TWELVE

Into the Dungeon

Soon though, Christmas Eve arrived.
Selena, Ella, Penelope, and Charlotte threw on splendid dresses. Oliver and Harry put on dress robes.

They went into the dining hall, which was spectacularly decorated. A deep blanket of snow covered the floor, and sparkling icicles hung from the ceiling. The giant evergreen was a fine addition to the strings of holly and pine lining the walls. The hall was lit by one huge torch. Charlotte looked at the exact replica of the torch of the first Olympic games with admiration. Two long tables were placed in the dining hall, and many students were already sitting there. But now, students from all the different groups sat together, chatting merrily.

In front of the two long tables was the staff table. All the teachers were looking cheery, except Tantalus, who was grimacing. As Penelope sat down, he threw her a look of disdain before glancing up at the ceiling.

Charlotte frowned. A bright idea lit up in her mind. She jotted it down and stuffed it into her bag.

They sat down. Suddenly, a menu appeared in front of each of them. "Fancy!" giggled Selena as she picked up her menu. Once Ella had decided, no food appeared. She looked up at the staff table.

Professor Watonburn smiled and scanned his menu carefully. Finally, he said to his plate, "Mashed potatoes!" Mashed potatoes appeared on his plate.

Everyone took this as the cue to start.

Suddenly, the hall was filled with voices shouting their preferred dishes to their plates.

"Pork Chops!"

"Onion soup!"

"Spaghetti and meatballs!"

"Lasagna!"

"Roast Chicken!"

"Christmas here is so jolly!" Penelope said.

Charlotte looked at her empty goblet, and she looked down at the menu once more. It listed a great variety of drinks.

"Orange juice!"

Sure enough, that's what appeared.

After the food, Professor Watonburn waved his wand and the tables disappeared. They played some Christmas snow games in the enchanted snow in the hall. Some of which were very dangerous, such as tobogganing down a hill, and some very funny, like throwing pie at Tantalus's face.

Ace was also staying at Mountain View for Christmas. During break, the students were excused from the usual black uniforms, and so Ace was once again sporting his letterman jacket. When it was his turn, he carefully selected a pie and clasped it tightly in his right hand. In front of all the onlookers, he narrowed his eyes and took aim. A moment later, Tantalus's face was covered with cream.

Tantalus was forced to endure two more rounds of this, for both Ella and Harry took part in this game, though neither of their aims was as good as Ace's.

The Professor scoffed and scowled, and after his turn, he marched right up to Professor Watonburn, wiping his face on his robes, and demanded that this game be removed next year while lemon meringue dripped off his chin.

"You look very nice, Professor," Charlotte told him.

"Shut up, fatherless girl," he responded, and cleaned his face with his wand. At once, his entire countenance became much more intimidating.

Afterward, they quickly ran back to their dorms and piled up their presents. Professor Watonburn said that the Mountain View servants would collect them in the night and deliver them.

It was dusk. "One of the things Mountain View does during the holiday week," Professor Watonburn said, "is stargazing." The auroras were on display, and with the Professors' permission, most students chose to camp out that night.

"They'll freeze to death!" said a surprised Oliver when he had heard the news.

"But we can do magic!" Charlotte explained excitedly as she pulled up her sleeves and flicked her wand. "Flame!" she cried, and bright orange flames burst out of the tip.

After convincing Oliver to camp out with them, they conjured a tent and pulled on their warmest clothes. They brought sleeping bags stuffed heavy with wool and camped outside in the snow. With their sweaters and coats on and the fire blazing in front of them, it was not cold at all, and they watched the aurora.

A blaze of green followed a mixture of pink and gold. It was very beautiful.

"Are those natural or enchanted?" asked Selena, as she admired the way the colored stripes swam and twisted in the sky above them.

"Enchanted, of course," replied Charlotte, also gazing, awestruck. "Colorado isn't far enough north to get the northern lights naturally, these must be put here through spells."

"Yeah," breathed Harry. He wasn't quite as interested in this "Christmas lightshow" as Selena, but he still enjoyed them, it was evident from the look on his face.

Penelope sat with them, equally awestruck, as the *Aurora Borealis* shone above them. One moment, there were two parallel stripes of pink and green. The next moment, they had wound their way through the heavens like serpents, fading into a dazzling purplish-blue mixture, curling into a circle. They flickered a few times and began shape-shifting again.

"They're wonderful," agreed Oliver.

"Have some hot cocoa and Christmas cookies," came a soft voice.

A girl with a short brown bob approached them. Charlotte was sure she had seen her somewhere before.

"Effir Hosanna," whispered Ella.

Charlotte suddenly knew where she saw her.

"Hi, Effir!" she said cheerily. "Merry Christmas, and don't miss the carriages next year!"

"Merry Christmas back!" she said. "And, alright, hopefully my brother will have grown up a little. You mind if I sit with you?" she asked.

"No, we don't mind!" said Ella. "Come join us! What's the matter? Friends went home for the holidays?"

"Nope," she said as she sat down on the snow. "I don't really have friends. They think I'm sort of an oddball, you know. But I don't really care. Hot cocoa, Charlotte?" she asked as she passed a mug to her.

"Thanks, Effir," Charlotte said. "How come they think you're an oddball?"

"Many reasons," she replied without a hint of annoyance or sadness. "As you saw back there at the carriages, I'm a bit of a klutz. I'm kind of awkward and weird and all those things. Don't worry though, I'm fine. Mountain View is fun, and I've never really felt lonely."

Charlotte sipped her cocoa uncomfortably. "Oh, well I guess I see. So, Effir, will you stay with us tonight?"

"Yes, I shall, if you don't mind. Thank you," she replied.

Ella smiled.

"Games?" offered Oliver, unearthing a chess set from his backpack.

"Oh, yes!" agreed Ella.

They sat down and divided into pairs, and the games began. After an hour of various magical board games, they had smiled until their cheeks were aching and quite sleepy.

Effir yawned. "You know, papa says sleeping alone on Christmas will land you more presents. Well, Merry Christmas!" Effir said as she took her tray of cookies and hot cocoa and jumped up to go offer one to Professor Historic, who was out patrolling between the students, and currently breaking up a rowdy snowball fight between Ace and Jude.

"Effir is a bit weird," commented Oliver, as he watched Ace hit a perfectly on-point snowball at Jude's face.

"Er...yeah," said Charlotte. "I feel bad for her not having friends though."

"Agreed."

"But she seems ok," added Charlotte as a second thought. "As long as she's happy, I guess."

"I'm freezing!" Penelope said.

"Oh, okay," Charlotte said while looking at the bonfire. It had gone out, and a thin layer of snow had powdered the top. She siphoned off the snow and muttered "fire" again, and the flames leaped up to warm them. A sleepy silence drifted across the night.

Suddenly, the idea that occurred to Charlotte in the great hall came back into her mind.

"Penelope?" she whispered, turning around. But Penelope was already fast asleep inside the tent. She turned the other way. Harry and Selena were fast asleep as well. So was Oliver, only Ella was still awake, groggily fumbling with a few chessmen. She looked up as Charlotte said Penelope's name.

"Hm?" she asked.

"Nothing," replied Charlotte. She decided it was best to wait until tomorrow to ask her. "Let's go to bed!" she concluded, extinguishing the fire.

"Hey, hey! Wake up! Presents!" somebody shouted.

"Wha—oh, morning Harry."

Morning light was already filtering through the windows, and Harry was the only one awake. He was shaking a box labeled with his name. Ella, Selena, Oliver, and Penelope were, like Charlotte, yawning and just getting up.

Charlotte looked through the tent window. It was all white.

She pulled on her sweater and snow pants. "Er, Harry, why's it entirely white outside?" Charlotte asked, picking out the biggest of her gifts.

"We got snowed in!" he explained. "Because of me."

Charlotte looked bewildered.

"Because I'm Harry *Snow*!" he said, laughing, unusually cheery. He passed an orange box to Charlotte. "This is yours!"

Charlotte smiled and proceeded to unwrap the box.

"Well, we did get snowed in," continued Harry. "So much, that we're buried!" he gestured to the window on top of the tent. It was all white as well.

Charlotte grinned as she tore open the wrapping paper. She looked inside. There was a card and a box. She picked up the card and began to read.

To Charlotte:

Merry Christmas to one of my best friends! Charlotte, you are kind, smart, and have a wonderful personality. I'm glad to be your friend, and I hope you like this! It's a wand-polishing service kit, I placed an order with a pigeon and it was delivered last week through EPD. It contains special wand sanitation wipes, polish, wood filler, and tweezers inside. Well, Merry Christmas!

Selena

Selena had just woken up and joined them. Seeing what was in Charlotte's lap, she grinned.

"Thanks!" Charlotte told her. "I bet it'll be very useful."

"No problem," replied Selena.

"What's this EPD?" asked Charlotte as she picked up another box labeled with her name.

"Express Pigeon Delivery," replied Selena. "It's a wizarding postal service, they deliver with pigeons."

"Wow, what're these?" came Harry's voice.

Charlotte looked up. Harry was clutching a bag of Charming Pets: Exclusive Chews.

"Hope Comet enjoys them," explained Charlotte. "They were the exclusive new chews that just came out last week. I managed to order one, I saw the ad in the newspaper."

Ella turned back to unwrapping her own presents.

"Make it snow more," Penelope suggested Harry.

Harry grinned.

"*Snow!*" He jabbed the tip of his wand at the tent. Instead of making it snow, it shook off the snow already on top.

"Snow!" Harry commanded again.

A single snowflake drifted down. They laughed.

"Not a bad haul," Charlotte said as she indicated the pile of things beside her. Besides the wand service kit, she also got an ancient book from Professor Watonburn called *The Dark Arts Not Yet Vanquished*.

It's an ancient and rare book, he explained in his note. *Use it well.*

Ella got Charlotte a whole new bundle of quills, parchment, and ink; Harry gave her a Fortune-telling crystal ball; Oliver gave her a chess set; Penelope gave her blue matching sweaters (one was for her, and one was for Penelope); Mr. Lexington sent her a simple card with one line of holiday greetings; and Mrs. Ross had sent her a hand-knitted scarf.

She was ready to get up and leave for Christmas breakfast.

"Alright, let's go," said Charlotte, wrapping a scarf around her neck. She stood up and unzipped the tent.

BA-BOOM!

All the snow had caved in. It didn't matter to Charlotte. "Flame!" she cried, pointing her wand at the wall of snow still obscuring the way out. Bright blue flames leaped from her wand and melted the snow in a second. She gave her wand a complicated little twirl and dried off her robes before marching away.

They walked inside the entrance hall, leaving wet mushy footprints behind them. Slipping and sliding, they entered the hall and sat down at their respective tables.

"Cripes, I'm starving," said Harry as he pulled a large platter of scrambled eggs towards him.

Charlotte spooned some porridge into her bowl and began eating as well.

Once their breakfast was finished, they met up in the entrance hall for their day off.

Ella clapped her hands together. "So, what do we want to do today?" she beamed at them all.

"Let's go for a hike," suggested Harry. "It'll be fun in the snow!"

"Oh no!" Charlotte exclaimed.

"What, why?"

Ella turned and saw Charlotte, but she was not commenting on their conversation. She was hidden behind a newspaper.

"Look at this!" Charlotte said, lowering the paper and folding it so that they could see the headline: "Christmas Morning Fires Light Up Estes Park, Boulder, Longmont, and Louisville."

"Another fire?" asked Oliver worriedly, scrambling to see. "Which areas, did they say?"

"I hope my family's alright!" Ella said, tugging the newspaper out of Charlotte's hands.

"You'll be alright, Ella," said Selena. "Hermes Plaza is protected by magic. But my parents, they live south of Denver. Can you check?"

"This is outrageous!" Harry slammed the table, frustrated. "What's with these fires everywhere? Four fires in one morning?"

"I see you've seen the news," a deep voice sounded behind them.

Charlotte whirled around and saw Professor Watonburn standing there, looking immensely grave. "I have more news for the six of you."

"What?" Harry stood up. "Are... are our families like, I mean... are they alright?"

"Don't worry, Harry," Professor Watonburn assured him kindly. "All of your families are alright."

A collective sigh of relief sounded from five of them.

"Good," Selena said. "I should probably still write and check on them. Where else is evacuating?"

They burst into more frantic conversations. Ella almost made to leave the Dining Hall and go write a letter to her parents, but Professor Watonburn raised his voice.

"Please!" he said. "I must talk to all of you."

At once, there was silence.

"Ah, good," he smiled. "You see, as Mr. Snow was pointing out, there have been too many fires this year, all close together and very destructive. It is time I tell you—the Dungeon of Unknown Doom is located in Jurassic Park, Estes Park."

Charlotte and Ella gasped in unison.

"We went there, on our very first weekend here!" Penelope informed Professor Watonburn.

"You did?" he asked, suddenly stern. "Well, I'm glad you have returned safely. But I have not finished. This morning, a local resident called Dr. Lininger, who lived in the area, reported stirrings around the Jurassic bathtubs.

"Dr. Lininger is a retired physician, and his wife, Margy, was a nurse. Dr. Lininger is the president of the local HOA, and they are both very respected in the community. They are also very hospitable. One of his friends—Dr. Kading, another retired physician—visiting him in the chalet also testified for his report. I think it's safe to take their word.

"At five-thirteen in the morning, he reported seeing a dragon bursting from the bathtubs, I trust you know what those are?"

The six of them nodded their heads fervently, impatient for Professor Watonburn to continue.

"His account claims it is scarlet, and over eleven yards in length. It breathes fire. He says it just shot out from one of the bathtubs, perched atop a mountain, gave a roar, and started spewing fire every which way. He then took off, under the cover of night, to start fires all over Colorado. Dr. Lininger claims he returned around nine. I think this... this is your chance."

At midday, the six of them gathered in the entrance hall. Each of them carried a backpack, equipped with several bottles of water, a change of clothes, reference books, and lots of food.

They stood for a moment in silence.

"Ready?" asked Charlotte.

Harry cast them a dark look. "We can only hope."

Charlotte pressed her hand gently to the wooden doors, and magically, they swung outward, revealing a smoky sky and maybe a hundred people spread out on the front lawn. A blue carriage, like the ones that had carried them to the school, was parked there, four Pegasi already tethered. Professor Watonburn stood impressively in front of all this. He smiled encouragingly.

Charlotte glanced sideways at her friends. They nodded and proceeded down the stairs.

"Hello," Professor Watonburn greeted them at the base of the steps. "Well, this is the time. This is your hour. I have prepared a carriage. It will take you as far as Lily Lake. I'm afraid anywhere closer to the bathtubs would be too steep to land. Once there, I'm sure you will know the way.

"It is true, in fact, that I have many misgivings about sending the six of you, still underage, and with very little magical education, on such a perilous quest. But I do not have a say in the matter, the Dungeon chose you and your friends, Charlotte. So the least I can do is wish you all good luck."

At once, clapping burst out from the onlookers, many of them students, although Charlotte spotted the whole staff there, dotted among the crowd.

"In you get then," Professor Watonburn nodded, and pulled open the carriage door.

"Thank you, Professor," Charlotte said as she clambered in.

Once Selena, the last, had seated herself, Professor Watonburn shut the door and whistled. Immediately, the Pegasi started walking. They then broke into a trot, then a full-on gallop. With a moment's lurch, they spiraled into the grey sky.

Ella leaned out of the window to look back at the school. "No turning back now," she said.

"We will be alright," Penelope said reassuringly.

The carriage pierced the smoke and clouds, soaring from Longs Peak to Lily Lake in a matter of minutes. The four Pegasi circled the lake, checking that there were no people, and began descending.

With several *clinks*, the Pegasi's hooves landed on the ice. With a sickening *crunch*, the carriage followed suit.

The door opened, and Charlotte stepped out cautiously. She stomped and dug her heel in the ice experimentally. "It's ok," she called. "The ice is firm."

On that note, her friends followed her. The Pegasi stood waiting, snorting and coughing smoke and ash from their lungs. As soon as the last person was out, they gave an impatient whinny and flew away.

"Well, there goes our return ticket," sighed Penelope.

"Don't worry, we better get a move on," said Charlotte. "We'll worry about returning when we need to."

"Hello!"

They all whipped around and extracted their wands. A few feet away, on the bank, stood an elder. He took a few steps closer, but paused at the edge of the ice. He held up a hand in greeting.

"Hello there!"

Charlotte did not respond, wand aloft.

"I'm Tom Lininger, and I'm here to help at the request of Professor Watonburn!"

At these words, Charlotte finally relinquished her grip on her wand. She sighed in relief and called a greeting.

"Hi, we saw you in the news!"

"You are Charlotte? Great! And this would be, Ella? Harry? Oliver? Selena? Penelope?"

They all nodded in acknowledgement at the sound of their names. With another smile, Dr. Lininger said, "My home is a few minutes away, let us go there first."

They followed the elder, off the lake and into the parking lot. The only car there was a white Toyota 4Runner. Oliver glanced around apprehensively, no way the seven of them would fit in there at once!

But when Dr. Lininger opened the car door, it revealed an elongated seat that resembled a park bench, long enough for the six of them to sit on comfortably. However, the size of the car looked completely normal from the outside.

"Very cool car, Dr. Lininger!" Oliver said.

The six of them piled into the backseat, and Tom got into the front. They drove away from Lily Lake, and down to a place called Rambling Drive. Everywhere Charlotte looked bore signs of wildfire prevention. Trees had been cut down, leaves had been raked, and grasses had been pulled. Campsites have been closed and the whole landscape looked unusually barren.

As if reading her mind, Dr. Lininger said, "I will be very glad when the Dungeon is destroyed. The whole community has been having a very difficult few weeks, always worrying about the fires. We've been moving in and out at moments' notices, due to the sudden evacuation orders."

"We'll try our best, we promise," Charlotte said, leaning to the side as the car turned into the driveway. "We want this over with too."

"You are all very brave," Dr. Lininger told them as the car came to a halt.

They hopped out of the car, and ascended wooden steps that led up to a three-story chalet. Tom opened the door and immediately, a waft of warm air engulfed them, smelling like chocolate and blueberries.

Harry raised his nose excitedly, sniffing the air.

Inside was warmly decorated. One entire wall was devoted to glass windows that presented a magnificent view of Longs Peak, curtained against the blue sky. A fire was crackling merrily in the fireplace. Tom gestured for them to sit down at the dining table.

A moment later, an elegant lady walked in from the kitchen. She wore a flowery blouse and had short, permed blonde hair. She had blue eyes and was smiling warmly. In one hand, she bore a platter filled with blueberry muffins. In the other, she had a large pitcher of chocolate milk.

"This is my wife, Margy," Tom introduced her.

"Hello," Margy set the milk and muffins down. "Welcome! I made some blueberry muffins for you. Please help yourselves!"

She poured them each chocolate milk, and she and Tom took a seat at the table too. After thanking her, each of them grabbed a muffin.

"This is delicious!" Harry said. "That's by far the best blueberry muffin I've ever had, it's so light and fluffy."

After a quick snack, Tom pulled out a book from a shelf and set it down on the table. Charlotte quickly wiped her hands and leaned forward in anticipation.

"Here's the journal I've kept regarding everything I know about the Dungeon," he told them. "I've been keeping watch on it recently. Here's what I've seen.

"Firstly, the Dungeon entrance is through one of the Jurassic bathtubs, but of course, you know that.

"Secondly, there's a fire dragon in the Dungeon," he said. "If you've seen the news, you'll know all about it."

"Scarlet, over eleven yards in length," Charlotte filled in. "Yes, we heard."

"Excellent, well then, the fire dragon likes to emerge at dawn. Any time other than that, you can hear these deep, rumbling sounds at the top of bathtubs. They might seem to be coming from the wind, but they're actually the dragon's snores. A few expeditions has taught me that."

"I remember!" Oliver said. "And the wind was quite literally *roaring* too, I thought that was like, a dinosaur, because of the name."

Tom and Margy laughed.

"People have made a very close guess then," Tom said. "Alright, but I have not found an exit. I did some supersonic experiments, and it seems that the Dungeon trails on for over ten miles, so I hope you have enough provisions."

"I think we do," Charlotte said. "My strategy is to duplicate the food each time before consuming it."

"That's smart," Margy told her. "But it's not a straight path through. You might be held back for a while."

"There will be obstacles," Tom confirmed. "Sometimes there might be puzzles or things that require lots of time."

"We'll be fine," Charlotte said. "We already took leave of all our teachers."

"I won't mind taking some extra time off!" Harry blurted out. Tom and Margy laughed again.

"Do you have everything? Water, boots, jackets? We can always lend you some. The obstacles in the Dungeon are rather unpredictable. You could meet all kinds of terrain and climate, in one room."

"No, thank you so much, Dr. Lininger. We made sure to pack thoroughly."

"In that case, I'll drive you there," Tom said, standing up. "We better be off."

They all stood and made to leave.

"Thank you!" They all called to Margy as they left.

"After your expedition, you are always welcome here," Margy told them.

Harry stopped suddenly and doubled back into the chalet, grabbed another muffin, and pocketed it. He planned to ask Charlotte to duplicate it.

They returned to Lily Lake through the same path. Tom parked his magically enlarged car into the parking lot, and they all clambered out.

Tom escorted them around Lily Lake, and saw them to the foot of the mountain before finally saying goodbye.

"Good luck!" he told them. "And here's a tip: on the way down from the mountain, make sure to tie your boots up well, or your toes will knock against the front of your boots. Stay safe! Farewell!"

"Goodbye, Dr. Lininger," Charlotte called. "Thanks a lot for everything!"

With that, they waved and turned away.

Charlotte led them up the same trail to the top. The first part of the journey was smooth, for they utilized the trail set apart specifically for hikers. However, they then had to deviate from the trail and head up through the unmarked terrain.

Charlotte led, Ella and Harry close behind her. This time, of course, Ella was proceeding cautiously, testing each rock before hoisting herself upon it.

The six of them were all panting as they neared the top. Charlotte was stooped over low, using her hands to stabilize herself. Stepping over a large boulder, she turned and found herself at the very top.

A moment later, Harry appeared behind her, followed closely by Ella. The three of them looked back. Oliver, Selena, and Penelope were clambering up the dirt and rock path behind them.

When they'd all arrived, Charlotte proceeded to examine the two bathtubs.

"Which one?" asked Charlotte.

"And how do we get in?"

Ella grabbed a stone and tossed it into the larger bathtub. They waited a moment with bated breath, but nothing happened.

"Should we try the other one?" prompted Penelope.

Ella threw another stone into the second bathtub. For a moment, there was once again no reaction.

"Well, what other—!"

"ROARRRRRR!"

An earsplitting roar sounded from beneath their feet, unmistakably coming from the smaller one.

"Well that solves one mystery," Oliver muttered. "Now how do we get in?"

"Are you sure you want to know that?" murmured Selena timidly.

"Oh, come on," Charlotte said exasperatedly. "Guys, look. We don't have a choice. Trust me, this is not how I imagined my first year at Mountain View either, but we were chosen. We have a chance, a responsibility, to end this once and for all. Think about the families in danger from the wildfires now—your families too—and all the damage this horrid creature has done. Whatever is waiting for us in there, be it one dragon, or a billion; one hex or a hundred; one obstacle or a thousand, we owe it to everyone affected to try. So?"

Ella nodded. Harry was next. Selena, Oliver, and Penelope looked at each other then looked up determinedly.

"Good," said Charlotte, nodding approvingly. In a swift movement, she pointed her wand to the bathtub, and immediately, a whirlwind formed in the water, as if a stop had been pulled out of a drain.

The green water below them swirled and

Selena gasped. In a few minutes, the bathtub had been drained empty. Harry gaped at Charlotte. "How did you do that?"

Charlotte smiled mischievously. Slowly, she lowered herself into the bathtub. Her fingers dug tight into the crannies on the side of the rock. Carefully, she took a few steps and hopped down onto the bottom. "Let's go!" she called, and everyone followed suit.

In the middle of the basin, there was a circular hole.

"Looks fit for a dragon," Harry commented, and he cast the light charm. He peered down.

"I can't see anything," he reported.

"Well, only one way to find out," Charlotte hoisted up her robes and tightened her backpack straps. "Only follow if I call it's safe."

"Wait!" Ella dashed forward. "No, you can't go down there!"

"If I say otherwise," Charlotte said firmly, cutting across Ella. "Don't follow."

With that, she took a deep breath and slid feet-first down the hole.

Selena, Ella, Harry, Oliver, and Penelope waited anxiously. A minute passed. No sound.

Ella and Selena looked at each other.

"I'm going down there," said Penelope, but Harry threw out an arm and held her back.

"Let's wait a bit longer."

Five minutes. No word.

"Ok, enough," Ella said, and just as she was about to follow Charlotte, Charlotte's voice echoed up.

"It's ok!"

Selena let out a huge sigh of relief. "Go on, Ella!"

Ella disappeared out of sight, and Harry sat down next. "Talk about going down the rabbit hole!"

"Dragon hole," Oliver corrected him, sniggering.

It was very deep, and they each slid for about three minutes before being deposited at the very bottom. A kind of green slime covered the walls, making it very slippery.

The tunnel ended in a tall chamber, as large as a cathedral. The walls were all worn and chipped, the stone as jagged as knives. The rocks were also wet and moist, and the whole place reeked of mold and algae. Selena wrinkled her nose as she stood up.

"Somehow I can't picture a fire dragon liking this place," Oliver told Charlotte.

"Don't be deceived," she replied darkly, and once everyone had gathered, she led them onwards, wand held aloft, ready to strike at any moment.

They tiptoed forwards cautiously, ears pricked and eyes wide open.

After a short walk, they reached the opposite wall.

"It's a dead end!" Ella said, feeling the rough wall.

"Can't be!" Penelope exclaimed. "What will we do?"

"Charlotte, are you sure it was this bathtub?" Harry asked. "Charlotte?"

Charlotte did not reply. She was running a hand along the wall, her fingers traveling over each piece of stone. Her brows were furrowed in concentration.

"Charlotte?" Harry asked again, more urgently this time. "Are we in the right bathtub?"

"Oh, we are," Charlotte breathed as she stepped gingerly backward. "Run."

"Ok, I—what?"

"RUN!"

The six of them retreated hurriedly, and in good time. With an almighty groan, the wall moved. It slid backward and forwards, curling itself. Suddenly, the wall transitioned from the scales to a great, moss-green head. An enormous amber eye the size of a dinner plate blinked, and a roar shook the ground beneath them.

"The dragon!" Oliver shouted.

They all clambered back, hoping to escape up the tunnel, or at least hide out, but the tunnel had sealed itself. The dragon positioned itself and slithered out.

Its gigantic body was as thick as Selena was tall. It had smooth grey scales and spikes all over its snout. As it emerged, it unfurled its long, leathery wings, which even the cathedral-sized chamber wasn't big enough to accommodate. Its powerful tail thumped ominously on the chamber floor, and Ella started quivering beside Charlotte.

"Don't worry." Charlotte took a deep breath. "Keep your head, stay calm. Aim for the chinks in its armor, and if it breathes fire, roll out of the way and attack the inside of its mouth. The bottom of the belly also works. Anywhere exposed."

As Charlotte finished these words, the dragon roared and opened its mouth. Six hexes went flying into it immediately. Despite the peril of their situation, Charlotte was proud of her team, her friends.

The dragon spat and howled. It raised its head in agony as boils erupted on the inside of its mouth.

"Now!"

Ella, Charlotte, and Harry dashed to the right, Selena, Penelope, and Oliver to the left. The dragon turned its head, unsure where to attack.

Finally, it decided on its left. It crouched down and attempted to sink its teeth into Selena, but Charlotte distracted it by prying apart two scales and sending a scorching hex at the exposed skin. The dragon roared in pain and beat its wings, trampling around in fury.

Harry ducked and wound between the dragon's legs, baseball sliding under it and firing jinxes at the dragon's exposed underside.

But all they did was annoy the dragon terribly. He was not severely wounded, and try as they might, he would not succumb.

"We need to cast the paralyzing jinx on him together!" Charlotte said. Everyone, find a good clear target! On my count!"

They scurried around, finding loose chinks in the dragon's scales, or else standing in front of its mouth, or lowering themselves for an aim at the dragon's belly.

Charlotte was among those in front of the dragon. "One, two—!"

She fired a jinx at the dragon's eyes, and it roared again in fury.

"Three!"

As its mouth was exposed, along with its belly and uncovered areas, they each sent three paralyzing jinxes at him in quick succession.

His eyes snapped straight. He swayed on the spot, and Penelope ducked out from under him. With a *crash*, the dragon fell sideways and collapsed on the floor, legs, wings, tail, and mouth rigid.

"We defeated a dragon!" Harry exclaimed, awestruck by their own accomplishment.

"No way," Oliver grinned, nudging it with his toe.

"Yes, yes, well done!" Charlotte smiled encouragingly. "But we better keep going, we only paralyzed it, it should come back to its senses within the next fifteen minutes. I'm sure none of you wish to be present when that occurs."

So, they followed Charlotte onwards, through the hole in the wall and into the next chamber, where the dragon had formerly been curled up, sleeping.

As soon as they stepped over the threshold of the second chamber, a horrid smell reached them.

Ella gagged and immediately pressed the sleeve of her robe to her nose, trying to block out the scent. "What is that?"

Charlotte looked around, and immediately her question was answered. In a corner was piled several dead deer, which have obviously been there, rotting, for a long time. Bones littered the ground, and rats scurried under their feet.

"The dragon's leftovers," explained Charlotte. "Come on, we better keep going."

They passed from the second chamber of the Dungeon to the third. This one was incredibly long. Whether the effect was due simply to the heavy darkness, or it really was that long, they could not tell.

As they moved on, round silhouettes of what looked like hills passed into view. Selena squinted.

"What is this, hills inside a mountain?"

"I doubt they're natural," replied Oliver.

As they approached, Oliver was proven correct. The hills appeared to be made of trash and junk so that the whole place seemed to be a gigantic landfill.

Old refrigerators, smashed bookshelves, rusted automobiles, and torn clothing piled to the ceiling. Penelope walked with her eyes wide open, incredulous.

"How did all this get here?"

"Magic," breathed Charlotte.

As they continued on, they realized that the hills were not merely made of junk; there were some very interesting artifacts hidden in them.

Oliver spotted a gleaming, brand-new moped perched atop an old dishwasher; Penelope saw a glittering bust of King Tutankhamun that looked incredibly like the original; Selena found a gold necklace, set with pearls and lined with diamonds.

"Don't touch anything," said Charlotte darkly. "I think this is the test—temptation."

They carried on, occasionally stopping to admire something so intriguing they could not ignore it. Charlotte, in fact, saw a framed picture of none other than her parents. She recognized the face from the very few photos she'd seen of them, but she'd never seen this particular one. They were sitting at a table, a vase of roses between them, apparently at dinner.

Charlotte lingered for so long, taking in every detail of the picture, that Ella had to drag her away.

Finally, the end of the junk hills came into sight, and so did the end of the chamber. But this time, there was no door or exit in sight. It was a dead end.

"Don't tell me there's another dragon blocking the way," grunted Harry.

"These are brick, not dragon scales, that's for sure," Charlotte told him. "I think we've just got to find the way out somehow…"

Just then, a deep rumbling sounded behind them. The six of them spun on their heels and whipped out their wands.

The junk hills were coming alive, or so it seemed. The crests were rising as if something was stirring deep beneath them. Slowly, a rubber tire emerged from the sea of rubbish, followed by a bookshelf that was peeling and splintered in places. With an almighty heave, two broomsticks started waving in the air. Lastly, two refrigerators protruded.

This crude humanoid, created of junk, rose up three times Charlotte's height, dwarfing them.

It had a rubber tire for a head, a battered bookshelf for a torso, two broomsticks for arms, and two refrigerators for legs.

"What on earth?" screamed Ella as it took a clumsy step towards them.

"It'll be fine," said Oliver. "We can take this brute. We just defeated a dragon! I suppose we have to blast it apart. *Explode!*"

The jinx soared through the humanoid's empty rubber tire of a head. Oliver gritted his teeth and repeated the jinx. This time, it caught the junk humanoid in the bookshelf chest, but it rebounded.

"Duck!" screeched Selena, and they all stooped immediately as Oliver's jinx blasted into the wall.

"How is it doing that?" Harry asked, looking at Charlotte, who was quivering. "Charlotte?"

"It's unstoppable," Charlotte breathed, her voice unusually high-pitched. "A ricocheting hex is the most formidable and effective protection that can be placed on any inanimate object. It will not work for living beings, but for objects, any curse, jinx, hex, or spell will rebound off it, and any approaching weapons will be deflected. We can't do anything but run. Where is the only question."

"Why is it coming after us?" asked Penelope in a panic. "I bet it's because someone took something. Did anyone steal anything?"

All of them shook their heads, but Charlotte remained motionless, her head drooping, staring at her shoes.

"Charlotte!" exclaimed Oliver. "What did you take? How could you?"

Charlotte did not respond. Ella rushed over to her. The giant trash humanoid was five strides from them.

"What did you take? Throw it on the floor, maybe then he'll stop coming!"

Charlotte reluctantly extracted a folded-up piece of paper from her pocket. Ella took it gingerly and unfolded it. It was a photo, the very photo of her parents Charlotte had seen, smiling at the camera.

Ella patted Charlotte on the back and set the photo down on the floor. But nothing changed; the giant humanoid kept advancing.

They backed against the wall.

"Do we really have zero other options?" moaned Harry. "We can't all die like this!"

"I know what it wants," whispered Charlotte, and immediately all five heads turned. The junk humanoid was two strides away. "It was a sacrifice. It wants the life of the person who stole from the junkyard. Once I'm gone, you will be free to go. Now listen, once I'm gone, I suspect an entrance will open and you guys must—!"

"Oh, no way!" said Harry, blocking her as she made to run towards the junk humanoid. "You're the leader of this quest. We are lost without you!"

"There's got to be another way!" said Ella.

"I told you, there isn't," Charlotte responded. "Now, let me go!"

They pinned Charlotte against the wall. As they argued, Charlotte attempting to break out of her friends' binds, the clunking of the junk humanoid's approaching steps stopped. They all relaxed their grips and looked on, bewildered.

But what they saw made all of them cry out. Selena, all alone, was at the feet of the junk humanoid, and she had opened one of its refrigerator legs. The door of the refrigerator swung on its hinges in what was unmistakably a beckoning wave.

"Selena, no!"

But sacrificing herself was not Selena's plan. In one hand, she clasped a squirming rat. Selena looked revolted, but she bent down and flung it into the refrigerator, then snapped the door shut behind it.

At once, the humanoid swayed, and then its knees buckled. It collapsed face-first into the ground and stayed there, unmoving.

"Selena!" gasped Harry, evidently impressed. "That was brilliant!"

Selena smiled. "The junk humanoid won't know the difference, it probably can only sense a life was placed inside it, and that was good enough."

"Thank you," Charlotte told her, bowing her head. "I'm sorry, that was so stupid of me and—"

"Hey," Selena coaxed her. "I get it, totally. If it were my family..."

She trailed off, but the two of them stared at each other in silent understanding.

"Hey, where'd the rat come from?" asked Ella.

"Well, this place is truly a dumpster, and with dumpsters come rats. I thought there must be some around here. I performed a summoning charm and then came this little guy." "That was brilliant!" Penelope told her. "Genius."

The rest of the day passed uneventfully. Charlotte was right. Once the junk humanoid collapsed, a doorway had opened on the bleak brick wall. They passed through it, and after an hour or so of walking, downcast, Charlotte yelled in pain.

She stumbled backward, her hand pressed to her forehead.

"What's wrong?" Penelope asked, the silence finally broken.

"There must be a barrier here," muttered Charlotte, reaching forward with one hand, the other still rubbing her forehead.

Her outstretched hand groped for the invisible wall, and at once, she felt it.

"It's definitely here alright," she said, half-heartedly. "And probably concealing more danger. My watch says it's eight o'clock now. How about we just kip out here for the night. I've got some burritos for dinner."

They set up camp, basically meaning they unrolled their sleeping bags and set down their backpacks. Charlotte passed around burritos, and they sat and ate quietly. After dinner, they went to bed early, exhausted.

But there was no snoring, and each of them turned restlessly in their bags. Charlotte lay awake, staring at the ceiling until past three in the morning. Then, she finally fell into an uneasy sleep.

She awoke with a start. Roaring and stomping could be heard behind her, where they had come. She looked around. All of her friends were awake and staring toward the direction of the noise tentatively.

"The dragon's come out of the paralyzing jinx," said Charlotte, leaping to her feet with renewed energy. "We have very little time. Now, you guys pack up, let me see how I can destroy this barrier."

In the face of this new peril, Oliver, Selena, Penelope, and Ella rolled up the sleeping bags, and Harry stuffed them into their backpacks. Charlotte was running a finger up and down the barrier, an open book in her hand, deep in thought.

When finally, her friends had packed and were waiting expectantly for her to make a move, she snapped the book shut and murmured, "Yes, I think that will be it. Stand back now."

They retreated a few steps, and Charlotte flicked her wand. "*Shatter!*"

With a loud *crunch*, a crack appeared in the barrier, quickly spreading, weaving, and forking, like a spider web being woven in time-lapse.

When at last a mosaic had been formed, the barrier burst outwards, glass raining down upon them. They all instinctively held up their arms to shield their faces from the splinters of glass that showered them.

They dashed across just as a roar sounded behind them. On the other side, Charlotte held up her wand and waved it at the barrier, *"Repair!"*

The barrier rose up and pieced itself together, as if it were simply a very intricate puzzle. Just then, the dragon appeared on the other side. Abandoning all pretense, the six of them broke into a sprint, dashing the other way. In time, they had reached the next chamber.

As soon as they entered through the circular entranceway, the gate sealed itself.

"Hey!" Harry shouted, banging on the wall. They turned to see the other end of a chamber. It was sealed, and they were trapped.

A piece of parchment materialized at Charlotte's feet. Cautiously and curiously, Charlotte bent and picked it up. It read:

Stranger, in this room, you must find five descendants of Arachne.
Collect them all, and then another clue will appear
to help you to the next obstacle.

As they looked up, the room suddenly began to expand. It continued to enlarge and become bigger until it was ten times its original size.

As Charlotte turned around, the rock began to carve nooks and crannies into itself, so that it turned into a very rough cavern. Charlotte began to lose hope with every new nook.

BAM. The lights went out. They moved around in the dark, but nothing else happened.

"Light," they all whispered.

"What are the descendants of Arachne?" asked Selena.

"Arachne was the weaver who challenged the Greek goddess Athena to a weaving competition," Charlotte said, her eyes closed in concentration. "And, after she won, Athena turned her into... into... a spider! That's it, there are five spiders in this cavern, and we've got to collect them!"

"Good. Now, let's find those spiders," Ella said.

They searched for half an hour and managed to get one spider. Penelope saw its black exoskeleton glimmering with the light from her wand. She originally thought it was a piece of mineral embedded in the rock, but then it scampered. She quickly slammed a hand over it, cupping her palm and trapping it. Charlotte put it in an empty jar, and they took a drink of water before continuing. By the end of that day, they had found another spider.

They went to bed, exhausted. Charlotte woke up first the next morning. When Selena and Harry woke up, they warmed their breakfast with magic, and the smell of breakfast burritos must have woken up Oliver, Ella, and Penelope.

They ate, and then they continued searching. But they didn't have any luck. It was extremely difficult to move in this cavern, due to the stalagmites that were growing up from the floor in front of their very eyes. The walls were made of extremely sharp rock as well, so it was difficult to feel around the small nooks.

They managed to find a third spider, but that was by the end of the day. They'd gotten so tired they didn't do anything the next day, but merely chatted and played some games.

Charlotte suddenly stopped feeling well. She began to vomit constantly, and couldn't go to sleep. She had a fever and wouldn't eat. Penelope knew the most about magical remedies, and she stopped to care for Charlotte.

There was more bad news because Oliver usually wore glasses, but he'd trampled them in the scurry from the junk humanoid. This severely impacted his ability to see and, therefore, search for the spiders.

So, Ella, Selena, and Harry were the only ones left. They searched, but their mind was on Charlotte. This happened for an entire week. Since they were preoccupied, they only found one spider.

"What's the point?" asked Ella, tired one night. "Even if we get the stupid spiders, it'll be hard to move Charlotte out of this cavern."

"Burt vee cannot just sday 'ere our 'ole lives!" croaked Charlotte.

"Oh, fine!" said Ella unwillingly.

This pattern continued for another week, and the tension inside the cave was building up.

"I'm not continuing!" said Harry one day.

"Ay, Harry," Charlotte croaked, turning to look at him, and attempting to prop herself up.

"Whoa there," said Penelope, forcing her back down. "Don't push yourself."

"Yes, yes," Charlotte said impatiently, looking at Harry. "Listen, Harry. We have to get the spiders, or else we will all die in here!"

"Yes, but how?"

"Harry, leesten and follow what I say," Charlotte gasped. "Try, try a summoning spell. Just 'old yer wand out and say, say '*summen spidah!*'"

Harry nodded and followed Charlotte's instructions. A moment after he said the incantation, a tiny spider zoomed headlong onto his hand.

He jumped with fright and quickly dumped it into the jar with the three other spiders.

"Yes!" Ella jumped up in delight. "We did it! We got the spider!"

Before they could celebrate, Charlotte descended into a violent fit of coughs. Penelope rushed over to her and patted her back soothingly.

But as Charlotte's coughs ceased, she was able to sit up and then stand up steadily.

"That must be part of the Dungeon's curse!" Charlotte said. "I'm alright now. Harry, Oliver, that was brilliant!"

The six of them high-fived each other exuberantly, and a second sheaf of parchment appeared on the floor. Charlotte picked it up and unfolded it. It read—

Congratulations on acquiring the spiders. You are almost at the end.
There is but one more obstacle before you may go.
Can you best this?

In a flash of blinding white light, the six of them were transported away from the chamber and into yet another.

This chamber was not very tall, but it was enormous. Charlotte once again could not see the end or either side. Other than that, it was essentially the same as everywhere else they had so far visited inside this depressing Dungeon.

"We finally did it," remarked Penelope. "After all that time, we finally learn we could've done it in about three minutes."

"Good for us," said Charlotte, smiling. "Shall we call it a day?"

They set up camp, rolled out their sleeping bags, and Ella illuminated a magical fire in front of them for warmth. Charlotte pulled up six stale cheese sandwiches from her bag, but before handing them out, she duplicated them and put the clones inside her bag.

"We've got to use any means we can to get enough food," said Charlotte. "This is most certainly taking much too long."

They ate dinner in high spirits, elated by their recent success. Shortly after dinner, they went to sleep. Tired by the day's events, they fell asleep quickly.

Charlotte felt as if she had barely closed her eyes before she awoke.

She looked around, wondering what it was that had caused a commotion loud enough to wake her. But all was quiet and still, her friends were snoring beside her.

Charlotte glanced down at her watch, pushing her hair out of her eyes. It was barely six in the morning. She could not see why she had suddenly decided to wake up.

Wondering in frustration whether or not she would be able to fall asleep again, she looked around at her sleeping friends, their torsos falling and rising rhythmically.

Then, out of the corner of her eye, she saw something.

"Wake up!" she bellowed, shaking all of them. There, striding towards them, was the most evil-looking woman Charlotte had ever seen.

They all started, stood up, and raised their wands in defense of themselves.

"Dagina!" they all cried in unison. Despite never having seen her, or even a picture or portrait of her, they all instantaneously knew who she was.

She drew nearer, smirking. Dagina wore a *chiton*, but it was black instead of the traditional white, trimmed with gold lace. It billowed out behind her extravagantly so that it made her look like a large bat when she walked. A wreath of golden laurels had been placed over her curly dark hair. Her lips were scarlet, in her eyes shone maniacal laughter.

She surveyed them carefully, and when her eyes met Penelope, they widened.

"Working against me now?" she smirked. "Found yourself a couple of good friends and settled down, didn't ya, Penelope? What happened to Sam and Bob? I cannot deny that they were *quite* useless though, slumping around like that!" She gave a high-pitched, shrill cackle.

"Dagina! How come?" asked Oliver. And then he remembered what Ella said Penelope told her when Penelope first joined them.

"So, this is where you've been hiding!" said Oliver.

"How dare you speak to me like an equal?" cried Dagina. "I am no equal! I am better, stronger, and different from everyone else! And call me by my name, did you? Show some respect!" She flicked her wand, and Oliver began to thrash and scream.

"No!"

Charlotte, Selena, Ella, Penelope, and Harry started towards her, firing hexes one after another in quick succession. However, with a sweeping movement from her wand, a black shield made out of smoke appeared in Dagina's hand. Though it seemed quite insubstantial, it repelled all of their spells, and the jinxes merely glanced off its surface.

As her friends continued to put up a valiant fight, Charlotte circled around the back and ended up behind Dagina. As she was not looking, Charlotte signaled to her friends. Harry spotted her and nudged Penelope. They passed the message on slowly, and just as Ella got wind of it, Charlotte whipped her wand and shouted, *"Explode!"*

The ground under Dagina blasted apart, throwing her off her feet.

"Freeze!" cried Ella, Oliver, Selena, Penelope, and Harry in unison, with a few milliseconds of difference in between. Dagina blocked all of them with ease. They rebounded, and Ella had to duck.

"Humph! Kids! They know what the good call *teamwork!*" came a different scathing voice, this one male. "They'll learn soon enough that other people can only get them so far, the only one you can truly rely on is yourself."

They turned around to see a troop of witches and wizards marching towards them. They were all wearing black wizard robes, unlike their eccentric leader, Dagina. They covered their faces with hoods, and they marched towards them orderly, converging around their leader.

They encircled them.

The six spread out, and facing outward, they aimed their wands at as many of them as they possibly could. They rotated, around and around.

Finally, Charlotte decided to act. She took out a pouch from inside her pocket and dumped it on the floor. Immediately, a kind of smog arose from the ground up, and the world went dark.

There were muffled shouts from Dagina and her followers.

"Here!"

Charlotte grabbed her friends by the wrists. They didn't know how she was able to see, but they didn't ask in this time of danger. She pulled them back towards the camp, and with one wave of her wand, packed up everything, and helped her friends put on their backpacks. By now, the smog was clearing. Charlotte threw just another pinch of powder, and then, they were engulfed once more by darkness.

Charlotte , being able to see, led them out of the darkness and back into the sunlight. They ran. They ran and ran and ran. Looking back, Charlotte saw that a whip of pure fire was thrashing around behind them through the smog. Whenever it touched the black fog, it evaporated.

Charlotte averted her eyes from Dagina and pushed them to continue to run. They sprinted maybe a mile or more. They ran all the way until it was impossible for Dagina to see them.

"I want to get out of here as soon as possible," Charlotte said, panting hard, doubling over and clutching her chest.

"You know, we're just a bunch of nine-year-olds, why should we continue? Shouldn't we just leave it to more experienced wizards to do the job?" asked Ella wearily, wiping beads of sweat off her forehead.

"*Resilience, Ella! Resilience!*" said Charlotte. "This obstacle is supposed to make us think this!"

Ella sighed. "Alright..."

"Yep!" Oliver said. "But it's kind of odd, you know? Dagina is supposed to be the evilest witch or wizard that's ever lived, and we just defeated her like that!" He snapped his fingers.

"Oliver," Charlotte shook her head, "We didn't defeat her, we ran. Besides, I think she's biding her time in the dungeon. She would come out if she was powerful enough."

Suddenly, they stopped. Charlotte, of course, had noticed something strange on the sand. Cookies, chocolate chip ones, were lying in a line on the ground.

"Ooh, nice! This Dungeon rewards you!" said Oliver, picking one up.

"Don't eat it!" shouted Charlotte, snatching the cookie away. "It's very likely to be a trap." She eyed it suspiciously.

"Eat! Eat! It's no harm at all! Eat!" came a very shrill voice.

Apparently, Charlotte knew what was happening a split-second before it happened, and she produced six earmuffs and snapped them onto everyone's ears. But, in her quickness, Oliver's earmuffs weren't tight enough, and they fell off.

"Eat! Sooo delicious, why refuse?" asked the voice, but of course, only Oliver heard it.

He rolled into a trance. His eyeballs had a dreamy, far-off look. He picked up a cookie, but his eyeballs were looking straight forwards.

Charlotte moved fast and knocked the cookie out of his hand. It landed on the floor. He went back for it. Charlotte reached for it at the same time—

CHOMP!

"OUCH!"

Who knew how aggressive this trance had made Oliver! He had bitten Charlotte's finger, and quite hard too. It was bleeding profusely, so everyone did what they thought was best. Penelope smartly summoned all of the cookies and held them, waiting for Oliver's approach. Ella fixed Charlotte's broken finger, Selena was standing to the side, and Harry tried to restrain Oliver and almost got his arm taken off.

Charlotte had come back to her senses. Oliver was rounding on Penelope. She did some quick calculating and summoned the cookies into her arms, and Oliver turned away from Penelope. Moving fast, she destroyed all of the cookies with a rather loud blast.

Oliver came out of his trance and looked at Charlotte's bandaged finger. He stared at his shoes.

"I'm sorry," he whispered.

"Don't be! Nonsense!" said Charlotte firmly. "It was my fault. I didn't snap your earmuffs on tight enough."

She summoned all of their earmuffs and put them away.

Suddenly, there was a large *CRACK!* Thirty or more people surrounded them. Charlotte knew what was happening. So did everybody else.

"Freeze!" they all cried and pointed their wands carelessly.

After facing Dagina the first time, they had planned out their attack formation. It was basically to fire off the most dangerous spells and hexes carelessly, but there was a catch. They all had their backs to each other, and no one was allowed to fire a jinx behind them.

"Faint!"

"Freeze!"

"Disarm!"

"Flame!"

There was an endless chorus of incantations, and it seemed that all of Dagina's followers were too stunned to react. Charlotte and her friends spun around and around, firing off jinxes. Finally, almost everyone was down except Dagina, who continued to stand tall and regal.

"So, you've got a plan," she cackled, and with one flick, she sent a ball of fire hurtling through the air towards them. They ducked, and the formation broke, and they scattered. She laughed again.

Then, Oliver and Penelope snuck behind her the other way and tried to hex her.

She blocked every hex, jinx, and curse the six threw at them with ease, managing to fire some of her own at them when she got the chance.

Finally, Dagina seemed to have had enough. She let her wand relax, and she tilted her head upwards, closing her eyes serenely.

A transparent bubble climbed up around her. Charlotte sent every spell she knew at Dagina, but the bubble swallowed their energy.

Finally, Dagina waved her wand above her head, and all six of them fell down on their backs.

With another swish, they were immobilized.

"Now," Dagina said in a ringing voice, the bubble peeling off her. "Well, that was a valiant fight... for your age. Which was the one who tried the Killing Curse on one of my Grim Reapers?"

She looked at each of them in turn. They were all immobilized, so none of them spoke.

"Harry," she finally said. "I know it was you. You have fire in you, boy." She gave him an approving look. Harry glared at her to the best of his ability.

Now, however, I will show you the true extent of my powers."

She lifted her wand, and Selena began floating towards her. With a *thump*, Selena was deposited at Dagina's feet.

"I spare no mercy for any of you," Dagina shouted. "You are all but obstacles I can blast away. I fear no higher judgment and nobody can possibly defeat me."

Dagina looked at everyone present in turn. She turned and raised her wand.

"*Die*," Dagina whispered, pointing her wand at the cowering Selena. Within a moment, Selena's arm went limp. She collapsed. Dagina smiled at them softly, not a care for what she had just done.

"NO!" Charlotte broke free of the magical bind that Dagina had set upon her. Charlotte dove and grabbed her own wand a few feet away. Charlotte stood up.

"Come at me then," breathed Dagina softly. "Do you think you can win?"

"Selena!" Charlotte called. Regardless of everything around her, she dove towards Selena, right past Dagina.

Surprisingly, Dagina stepped respectfully aside.

"Selena," muttered Charlotte. "Selena!" Charlotte lifted Selena into her arms and checked her pulse. Her breathing. Her heartbeat. All negative.

"SELENA!" shouted Charlotte, shaking her as if Selena's corpse would wake.

Charlotte doubled over, clutching Selena's sleeve, sobbing into her hair.

Dagina watched with mock-pity behind her, twirling her wand relaxingly in one hand.

Charlotte's tears ceased, but she did not rise. She lay with Selena in her arms silently, unmoving.

Charlotte was in shock. Upon entering this Dungeon, she'd known there were risks and dangers awaiting her, but somehow, she never thought any of them would die. She might've voiced it to others, but she never believed it.

There was no way Selena could ever come back, even if part of Charlotte believed she would.

"You," whispered Charlotte in murderously low tones, not even looking at Dagina. "You killed her."

"Well, it took you a while to notice," replied Dagina, sounding somewhat bored.

Charlotte turned, still on one knee. Every part of Dagina, especially her regal and casual mannerism, angered her.

"You stand there like you just did nothing," muttered Charlotte with hatred. "I'll kill you for killing her!"

"Oh you'll try," sniggered Dagina, a sneer on her pointed face, not at all troubled.

"You think I'm afraid to duel with you?" asked Charlotte. "I have no hesitation."

"Oh, I'm sure," said Dagina, her casual tones disappearing now. She looked Charlotte severely in the eye and continued. "Take a word of advice from me, Charlotte. Righteous anger will not sustain you for long. So listen, take my advice, and be saved."

"I will," said Charlotte. "In your wildest dreams."

"Listen," continued Dagina, not at all discouraged. "You have just tasted something you've never had before. Death. It is inevitable. In the end, every one of your friends here will die, one way or another. Your mentors, your family. *Poof.*"

Dagina kept up her serious countenance. Charlotte glared back as fiercely as she could.

"If you think the ordeal you just went through was bad," muttered Dagina. "Think again. In life, you'll have to go through this over and over."

"What's your advice?" growled Charlotte. "I'm running out of time and patience here."

"Let go!" shouted Dagina. "That's it! Let go of emotion, of love. You cannot lose anything if you never had it. You cannot be sad if you never cared! My advice to you is this: Charlotte Isabel Lexington, join me! Join me! I will teach you to be cold, to let go of emotion! Live life without pain with me, Charlotte Lexington. You will be of great use to me at the same time. I have not killed you because you may be instrumental. You are not unintelligent. You have talent and wit. Use them to serve me, and I will give you true happiness in return."

Dagina's eyes burned with the same maniacal desire Charlotte saw when they first met.

"Join me..." Dagina crooned.

"If you think," muttered Charlotte, struggling to keep her tone even. "I will listen to you after you murdered my friend and tried to kill the rest of us, think again."

"Charlotte!" said Dagina again, in an exasperated tone. "I don't blame you, you haven't yet witnessed the labyrinth of suffering."

These words shocked Charlotte for a moment. Dumbstruck, she did not reply.

"Yes," said Dagina gravely, taking a step closer to Charlotte. "I am not evil, as the tales might suggest. I am merely helping you, I'm leading you, warning you not to go astray."

"I'm sorry," Charlotte said, coldly and firmly. "I think anybody who can murder a person without blinking an eye *is* evil."

With amazing agility, Charlotte leaped into the air, undoing the binding curse Dagina had put on her friends, and as one, they cursed her.

Dagina was not expecting it. Three curses caught her full in the chest. She tottered a moment on her heels, and then she fell on her back.

"Let's go!" yelled Charlotte, running off, trying to exercise the emotion out of her, transferring her energy to something else rather than dwelling on the pain in her chest.

As they ran, Dagina rose again. Ella pulled against Charlotte, wanting to go back to find Selena, but Charlotte tugged harder. Dagina sent a jinx at them.

Finally, everyone stopped struggling. As one, they ran as fast as they could away from Dagina, who was conjuring up dark storm clouds of fury above her.

"Come on!" Charlotte roared, and they sprinted away.

When Charlotte chanced a glance behind her, Dagina was holding up both arms to the sky, where layers of dark clouds were gathering. Beside her lay a limp Selena. The clouds covered them like a hat. Wind was blowing around Dagina; her robes were fluttering. Electricity crackled around her.

"Keep going," panted Charlotte, ignoring the ache in her calf, continuing to sprint.

Finally, when they were all panting fit to burst, and they could run no more, they collapsed onto the ground. Charlotte looked back. On the horizon, there was a patch of black, but that was all.

"Phew!" said Ella.

"I hope nothing worse can happen," said Charlotte, her tears returning.

It was late at night, according to Charlotte's watch. Charlotte and Ella cooked while everyone else pitched the tent. Nobody mentioned Selena, though everybody was melancholy, and Ella had tear tracks on her cheek.

"Time for dinner!" announced Charlotte half-heartedly as she split the macaroni and cheese onto each plate. With a start, Charlotte realized she had dished out six instead of five. Bitterly, Charlotte split the last serving amongst the other five.

They sat in continued silence. Charlotte spooned a mouthful of the creamy pasta into her mouth. It was tasteless. She managed to force down a few mouthfuls, and then she left them and went to lie down.

A few moments later, she heard another person softly clambering into the tent.

"Charlotte," Ella whispered.

Charlotte turned around, not having the energy to pretend she was asleep.

"Is… is Selena really gone?" asked Ella, tearfully staring at her.

Charlotte tried to say 'forever', but no words came out of her mouth. She settled for a nod, and then turned her head the other way.

"I—I never thought she would… that any of us would die on this adventure." Ella spoke the last words very quickly, as if trying to get the horrible ordeal over as quickly as possible.

"Me neither," whispered Charlotte, finally forming words. "And she was so young and innocent."

Penelope entered. She sat between Ella and Charlotte softly.

"I can't believe it…" muttered Penelope. "Gone? Like that?"

"I can't accept it either," said Ella.

Harry and Oliver entered together. They sat crossed-legged a little bit behind the girls.

"She was a nice friend," reminisced Oliver. "I knew her longer than any of you."

"She reached out to me," remembered Ella. "She was the first to make friends with me after I was sorted into second-tier. She came to me and tried to comfort me."

That night, they gently shared their memories of Selena. As Charlotte finally called for lights-out, she felt a lot better. The knot in her stomach loosened a bit, and she pulled the covers over herself with a melancholy smile.

The next morning, Charlotte awoke peacefully. It took her a moment to remember why she was feeling so miserable inside. When she recounted the loss of Selena, the agony was too much to bear, and she sat up.

"Awake?" a voice whispered behind her. Charlotte jumped and pulled out her wand.

"Whoa," whispered Ella in surprise.

"Oh, thank goodness it's just you," Charlotte stowed her wand back inside her pocket and sat down next to Ella. "You thinking about Selena too?"

Ella nodded. "I—I can't believe it, but we for sure can't dwell on it. That parchment, it said this was the final obstacle. We're so close, so close to finishing this place."

"Yeah, I've been thinking about that too," Charlotte said, furrowing her brows. "See, I thought we were here to destroy the Dungeon, like bring the roof down. Since when did we start doing this as if it were a mere obstacle course?"

"Maybe the way to destroy it *is* to beat it?" suggested Ella.

Charlotte shrugged in response. Just then, Oliver awoke, and Charlotte set about distributing breakfast—cheese sticks and bagels.

After everyone was awake and finished breakfasting, Charlotte broke camp for what she hoped was the last time in this Dungeon. She led her friends onward, slightly apprehensive.

After an hour of quiet trekking, they reached the end of the chamber. The wall was red brick, old, moss-covered, and crumbling in places. In it was set a metal door with a brass doorknob. Hoping this was it, Charlotte turned to look at her friends. They returned this gesture with an encouraging nod.

Charlotte reached out her hand, grasped the doorknob, and turned it.

The chamber beyond was pitch-black. It was so dark not a single thing could be spotted. Charlotte cast the light charm, but it barely illuminated half a meter in any direction.

Just as they were groping about in the darkness, a sudden flash of light appeared above them. They looked up, and there was a box, in which was a sword. It was the symbol of the Dungeon of Unknown Doom.

BANG!

Charlotte was thrown off her feet as the Dungeon's symbol exploded in a whirlwind of color. She landed hard on the floor and watched as a wave of some sort of energy swooshed over them.

"Charlotte," Penelope breathed. "Ella, Harry, Oliver..."

Ella stood up. She extended a hand to each of her friends in turn and hoisted them up onto their feet. As finally, Penelope was up, leaning on Charlotte, a ghost appeared, but she looked slightly familiar, somehow. "Jessica Aphelion!" whispered Ella.

She was the exact equal of Dagina, except with distinct differences. Her ghost wore a white chiton instead of black, her hair was blonde instead of black, and her eyes were soft, kind, and filled with pain instead of anger.

"I know, I know!" she said, looking down at her feet. "I never should've done it! It, it was just a sense of uncontrollable anger that made me!" she said.

"I know that happens," said Oliver.

"I understand," said Ella. Aphelion just sounded so sincere.

"I can give you only one warning: Dagina is not Jessica Aphelion. She is someone else, possessed, who sold her soul to the devil. Do not trust her. Do not pity her. Do not ever be soft with her. Please destroy her, little heroes. Destroy her. I'm so sorry..."

They nodded in understanding.

"We will," Charlotte assured her.

"And, I would like to grant you all each one wish," Aphelion added. "Congratulations."

Ella wanted Ace to turn into a toad for an entire day. Penelope wanted to never go back to her family. Harry wanted a new poster for his bedroom, and Oliver wanted a lifetime supply of hotdogs.

"You are all so tactless!" shouted Charlotte, stamping her foot.

"Ugh! Like you can do anything more tactful!" said Harry in an imitation of her voice.

Charlotte glared at him and leaned in towards the ghost of Jessica Aphelion.

"I want to meet my mother again, " she slowly whispered.

Jessica Aphelion spread her hands, and another ghost, this one taking the form of Olivia Lexington, appeared. She had soft, downy brown eyes and hair, which nearly reached her waist. Her eyes shimmered with happiness. She was a slim woman, wearing a delicate blue dress, which Charlotte identified as her mother's favorite one. She floated ethereally in the middle of the room, emitting a faint silvery glow.

Charlotte gasped, but she was not able to speak. She clapped her hand to her mouth in awe, staring wide-eyed at the silver figure.

Olivia Lexington opened her eyes and blinked. She looked around at Jessica Aphelion. "You!" she cried.

Jessica Aphelion bowed her head. "That was not me. That was a spirit taken over by evil."

Charlotte looked from Jessica to her mother, curious.

"What is this?" she finally asked.

"Charlotte," Jessica Aphelion shook her head, looking pensive. "It was Dagina that murdered your parents. You know about the Fog, right? It writes prophecies, then executes them. Your prophecy was made one year before your birth. The moment Dagina caught wind that the destroyer of her Dungeon was born, she set out to murder your family. It was Professor Watonburn who showed up on time to prevent her from finishing you as well."

Charlotte was silent, taking in this news.

"You've been so brave," Olivia Lexington whispered to Charlotte. "And you've done so much. I never knew you would make this good a witch!" She smiled sadly.

"You... you knew? You knew I was a witch? You knew I was magical?" stammered Charlotte, wonderstruck.

"Of course I knew. I was born to magical parents, yet I had no powers myself, no Micromaguses. It was an uncommon phenomenon. Your grandparents were disappointed, and ever since I grew up and became independent, I have never seen them again. Grannie Sarah and Grandpa Abram never visited you, I recall. Ah—if they knew. I do advise you to meet them over the summer. I think it would be pretty safe to assume that they will take an instant liking towards you once they find out you've been accepted into Mountain View and destroyed the Dungeon. They will read it in the Wizarding Post, a wizarding newspaper. They'll want to find you before you can even get home!" She smiled and stretched out her arms.

Charlotte slowly, hesitantly, reached out to grab hold of her mother's hand, but her hand only passed through her fingers.

Charlotte recoiled.

"Oh, dear. I will miss you," Mrs. Lexington said. "Be brave, for many things are in store for you in the future. Take care, Charlotte Isabel Lexington, good luck."

And before Charlotte could say a proper goodbye, her mother closed her eyes serenely, and tilted backward, floating away, getting fainter.

Charlotte felt tears welling up in her eyes. She sniffed and moved back to her friends. Ella squeezed her hand. Charlotte leaned against Penelope. Harry and Oliver offered their condolences.

They turned back to Jessica Aphelion. "Thank you," Jessica whispered. "Please, correct my mistake. Destroy Dagina. Thank you, you are more right than I have ever been."

She closed her eyes and faded away. The aurora-like symbol above her head also faded away.

Charlotte, Ella, Harry, Oliver, and Penelope looked at each other, assuring each other silently.

A moment's silence.

Charlotte turned to look at Harry from around Ella. "Was that more tactful?" she asked with a wry smile.

Harry laughed amiably. Not a trace of resentment.

As Charlotte reflected upon their journey through the dungeon, she felt like they had matured so much.

As if on cue, a bright light flashed. Charlotte shut her eyes in anticipation. They started spinning on the spot, not of their own accord. They whirled faster and faster, and finally, it felt as if they were being lifted into the air. With a faint *pop*, their feet touched the stone hallway of Mountain View.

THIRTEEN

Home

"Are you okay?" came a worried voice, as Charlotte stumbled, hitting the ground.

Mr. Lexington had hurled through the crowd to examine her. But she was so full of shock. She had seen her mother, her actual mother.

She also had, with the help of her friends, destroyed the Dungeon of Unknown Doom, a place teeming with dangerous creatures, dark spells, and Dagina herself. She and her friends had accomplished a thing that many full-grown witches and wizards have failed to do, and Charlotte was positively nonplussed.

"Are you okay?" shouted Mr. Lexington again.

"Wha—oh, yes. Stop shaking me, please!" shouted Charlotte, bursting into laughter.

It was bliss. She heard her voice reverberating off the halls, sounding sincerely happy. As she laughed, all of the pressure and anxiety welling up inside her came flowing out at once. She then groaned a little as she slowly laid herself down on the cold floor, tired and battered.

"What did you do? How did you make it out alive?" asked Mr. Lexington.

But Charlotte could only choke out three words with immense difficulty. "I saw Mum."

"What? Is there like a realm of the dead or something?" asked Mr. Lexington.

"No, there was no 'realm of the dead,'" said Charlotte. "I saw Jessica Aphelion, the creator of the Dungeon, and she granted us each a wish. I asked to see mum..." she could not say anything else.

"Ah... I do believe that our heroes need a rest. Good work," came Professor Watonburn's deep, calm voice. He smiled at them. "Congratulations. Oh, what an achievement for you."

Charlotte looked at her friends. Ella smiled at her. They exchanged a group hug.

Suddenly, Professor Watonburn asked, "Where's Selena?"

Charlotte took a moment. Then she turned her head and her eyes met Professor Watonburn's. She was silently pleading for him to understand.

He did. He nodded gravely and strode over to them, giving each of them a gentle pat on the shoulder.

By then, the word had spread that Charlotte and her friends had returned. Large crowds of curious students had gathered.

"Make way! Make way!" Professor Watonburn shouted. As they walked through the path that was cleared for them, Charlotte saw Tantalus's face among the crowd, looking terribly angry. His fists were balled up, and he was frowning and puffing, and his face was a deep scarlet. Charlotte could not help laughing a bit.

Then, the question that came to her at Christmas occurred to her again.

"Penelope, who was that spy?" she asked slowly and slyly.

"You guessed it, Tantalus!" she whispered back, laughing.

"Ah, Dagina will be perfectly—Dagina!" Charlotte suddenly screamed.

Everyone in the crowd gasped in alarmed unison.

"Dagina?" asked Professor Watonburn, turning around sharply and pointing his wand with a strong force.

"Where is she?" everyone asked frantically.

"No, we met her in the Dungeon!" said Charlotte.

"And you escaped?" asked Effir, her face popping out of the crowd. "Dagina is really powerful, and strong, and mad, and—!"

"Thank you *very much*, Miss Hosanna!" shouted Professor Starlight.

"Yiee—hahaha!" came a screech, and a red streak flashed past them. Everyone ducked as all the glass in the school shattered inwards. Then the streak disappeared.

"No!" everyone shouted in unison again.

"Well, there are more chances in the future to get her," said Professor Watonburn gravely. "And now I suggest we strengthen our defenses."

He began to twirl his wand and mutter incantations. "And Charlotte," he said, turning suddenly. "All of you, good job. Thank you." He smiled warmly at them again, and Charlotte fainted.

"Ah, time to go, Charlemagne," said a voice. Charlemagne was Charlotte's favorite nickname. It reminded her of the king. She wanted to do something as great as him.

"Uncle, are we leaving Mountain View now?" asked Charlotte groggily.

"Yes. The carriages are leaving in half an hour," he told her.

"How come? We've only been in there for a few weeks at most!"

"Oh, have you?" Mr. Lexington asked, slightly skeptically, as he straightened her suitcase. "It's been quite a while! Time must pass differently in the Dungeon. It's not unheard of."

Charlotte dressed and bounced down to breakfast. She paused before entering the hall.

"Charlotte! Here! Charlotte, behind you!" came Ella's excited voice. Charlotte turned around at once, only to see Ella, Penelope, Harry, and Oliver coming down the steps together.

"Oh, can you imagine the uproar?" asked Oliver dreamily.

For a split second, Charlotte saw herself walking down the aisle between the tables, the students cheering and applauding. She imagined the teachers' impressed faces.

"Oh, Oliver!" chided Penelope, bringing Charlotte back to firm reality.

"Come on," Charlotte whispered quietly to them.

As they went into the hall, every voice and sound stopped, though a few dropped forks and spoons clattered. They looked at each other nervously. Even the staff had begun to stare. Finally, Charlotte shrugged, and they took a step.

"YES!"

"WOO HOO! HOORAY!"

"YEAH!"

CLAP! CLAP! CLAP!

BANG! BANG!

The noise level was absolutely unimaginable. It was more than what Charlotte had pictured. Everyone clapped as hard as they could and banged the tables until their hands became scarlet. People set off fireworks, conjured birds, enlarged their voices, shouted, and Ella's eardrums were about to explode.

As the five of them made their way down the aisle to find an empty seat, they passed Amy Chase and Jenna Johnson, who were sitting next to each other at the second-tier table. Jenna waved enthusiastically, and both were staring at the five of them, glowing with admiration.

As they continued, Ace stood up on his bench at the second-tier table. He was already tall, but now he stood towering over everyone else. He was applauding with all his might, and he bellowed at Ella, "Now *that's* my sister!"

Jude stood up too and demonstrated his hearty approval of his best friend's sister with a loud series of whoops.

Finally, Professor Kitlowski, the math teacher, came down from the Head Table, arranging his glasses on his nose, and told the pair of them to sit down.

Eventually, it died off, but everyone was still talking and pointing. The five of them all took a seat at the top-tier table together, and nobody seemed to mind.

Only one person in the hall was looking terribly unhappy: Tantalus.

"Penelope, what about him? You know, him! *Tantalus*?" whispered Charlotte.

"Ah, I'll just go to Professor Watonburn—no wait, I can tell the entire school, and spill the beans," she said simply, and stood up.

The hall became quiet. Penelope took a deep breath.

"I don't want it to sound as if I were accusing anyone or anything, and I don't want to be disrespectful..." she paused, looking fixedly at Tantalus. His eyes enlarged with fear. "But Professor Tantalus apparently was helping my, er—family, and... Dagina!" A large gasp sounded, and in that split second, Tantalus stood and shaped into a cloud of black, crashing and escaping out of the windows.

"Thank you, Penelope," said Professor Watonburn grimly, repairing the window, "but I daresay he won't be back too soon."

Everyone returned to eating their breakfast, chatting excitedly and nervously. It was the end of an era. The era of Dagina's hiding. Now, she and her supporters were at large.

"Farewell, dear pupils," Professor Watonburn said at the station. "Have a good summer!"

"Bye, Professor W!" said Ace scathingly, tossing the football up in the air and then snatching it once more, but Professor Watonburn merely smiled.

"Ace, how dare you? He's the *headmaster!*" hissed Ella. Professor Watonburn had evidently heard but merely smiled again.

"I believe this is your last year," Professor Watonburn called back to Ace. "Unwilling though I might be to bid farewell to your lively presence at Mountain View School of Magic, I wish you the best in life with your many talents."

Ace's mischievous grin was suddenly wiped off his face. He pushed the football into Jude's arms carelessly, and walked up to Professor Watonburn. He held out his hand, and Professor Watonburn shook his hand seriously.

"Goodbye Professor," he said. Professor Watonburn returned a smile. Ace walked off and took his football back from Jude, a group of giggling second-year girls watching him.

"Wait, our end-of-year tests!" said Charlotte said to Professor Watonburn, right as she was about to board her carriage.

"Ah, Charlotte, the Dungeon was the most difficult test I could've given you. And I'd say full marks will suit you."

He handed her a piece of parchment.

She unrolled it excitedly. It read:

CHARLOTTE LEXINGTON ACHIEVED	
Charms	100%
Potions	100%
Astro-magic	100%
Transfiguration	100%
History of Magic	100%
Herbology	100%
Physical Education	100%
Language Arts	100%
Mathematics	100%
Advanced Spells and Curses	100%
History of Magic	100%

"Thanks, Professor!" nodded Charlotte.

"And bring these to your friends," Professor Watonburn said, withdrawing four more scrolls from within his robes.

Charlotte bade him farewell and leaped onto their carriage.

"Here, let me help you," Ella offered to help Charlotte pull her trunk onto the rack.

"Thanks, Ella," Charlotte said, patting it into a better position.

"What about you, Uncle?" Charlotte asked.

"I might sit up in front with Mr. Bromhead," he said thoughtfully, and moved away. "It'll be quieter there, I have a report—oh, I nearly forgot, I don't! You solved the wildfire problem for me!"

Charlotte and her uncle laughed in unison. Her friends clambered into the carriage.

"Well," said Charlotte, closing and locking the door.

"Why'd you lock it?" asked Ella, standing back up.

"Excuse me, do you expect nobody's going to try and disturb us?" asked Charlotte, lifting the window open. "Here's your end of year test grades."

"Oh yay," Oliver mocked.

"Open them," coaxed Charlotte, refraining from grinning.

"We'll all get T," Harry muttered dejectedly. "We didn't sit the tests at all!"

Charlotte finally succumbed to a smile as her four friends' formerly somber faces suddenly lit up with surprise. Harry's mouth fell open, and Ella squealed and began hugging everyone in reach.

After the shock of their exam results wore off, they began chatting. Halfway through an argument about who was the worst teacher now that Tantalus was gone, Harry pointed at the window.

"Hey, look at the pigeon!" shouted Harry, pointing at the bird that had landed inside their carriage.

He stuck out his foot to Charlotte.

"Er... thanks, little guy," said Charlotte, taking her letter.

"Open it," coaxed Ella.

"No, I'd rather have some privacy!" blushed Charlotte, having had an idea about its sender, recalling her discussion with her mother.

"Well, have it your way," Ella said, closing her eyes.

Charlotte flipped the letter over and gasped when she saw the sender's info.

Then, she smiled and tore open the letter.

It read:

Our wonderful Charlotte,

We never thought you'd be able to become a witch! Congratulations! But even more, we saw you in the Wizarding Post, and it was highly amusing to read of you destroying the Dungeon of Unknown Doom.

I can't wait to see you! Too bad Olivia didn't live to see you into Mountain View.

Love,

Grannie Sarah and Grandpa Abram

Enclosed was a newspaper clipping from that day's edition of *The Wizarding Post*.

Charlotte smoothed it out, propped it up, and began to read. Above the headline was a large wizarding photograph with subjects who moved.

It depicted Charlotte in the middle, Ella and Penelope on one side, and Harry and Oliver on her other side. They were walking uncertainly into the dining hall. Charlotte realized this to be taken that very morning.

The article read:

Dungeon of Unknown Doom Destroyed by Students
Marie Slick June 14th, 2021

In an astounding move last week, six Mountain View first-year students worked together to destroy the Dungeon of Unknown Doom, a dungeon harbored in the bowels of the Rocky Mountains. It was said it contained dark magic, cast by the mysterious dark witch Dagina. It was also rumored to be the hiding place of Dagina herself during those long periods in which she disappeared from wizarding society.

The five conquering heroes include Miss Charlotte Lexington, Miss Ella Ross, Mr. Harry Snow, Miss Penelope Brown, and Mr. Oliver Hayfield, all Mountain View first-years. Another girl, Miss Selena Caroline, reportedly entered in the quest with them, but she tragically died in the attempt.

In an exclusive interview with Mr. Alberto Vandenberg last night, owner of the wand shop Vandenberg's Wands in Hermes Plaza, he reveals that Charlotte Lexington and Ella Ross have all purchased wands from his store. "I was trying wands with Miss Lexington...and the logo of the Dungeon of Unknown Doom appeared out of the end of her wand...it is commonly accepted as the symbol of the Dungeon's selected destroyer..." he revealed.

In another exclusive interview with none other than the celebrated head of Mountain View School of Magic, Helios Watonburn, he reveals to us the obstacles that the five heroes had to get around in their quest, confided in him by Miss Penelope Brown.

"Miss Brown confided in me that they went through a number of obstacles during their journey. They battled a dragon, destroyed a humanoid created from junk scraps, encountered and battled with Dagina twice, and various other smaller tests.

"At the end, Penelope tells me they met the ghost of Jessica Aphelion before she became Dagina. Miss Brown tells me that Aphelion had told them to destroy Dagina, and that she had sold her soul to the devil. With that, they were transported back."

The Headmaster refrained from giving any information regarding the regrettable death of Miss Caroline in the Dungeon, although he assures me that he has properly informed her family and arranged her memorial service, naming her passing as "a regrettable accident."

The Headmaster also warns the Wizarding population gravely that once again Dagina is at large. He urges the community to stay alert and cautious.

Most of the wizarding community is still at shock over this news that five first-year witches and wizards have been able to destroy what many grown wizards could not.

"These astounding young talents should be expected to do something great in the future," remarked Mountain View Political Magic teacher Mr. Rufus Grayson. "While I have not yet had the fortune to teach any of them, for none of them have yet chosen my elective" —he chortled—"I reviewed all of their examination papers for their Mountain View Entrance Exams, and their respective Micromagus density counts and grades are truly something to be marveled at."

"Wow!" she whispered.

"What's so exciting?" inquired Penelope.

"Privacy?"

"Well, you're done with the letter, aren't—?"

"I said, ten minutes! I could be done, but ten minutes isn't up yet," Charlotte interjected. Ella raised her eyebrows and smiled.

"Have it your way."

"Grannie Sarah and Grandpa Abram are visiting for the summer!" Charlotte finally said, when she had folded up the letter and processed it all through.

"I would like to meet them, they sound friendly," said Penelope.

"And look at this!" Charlotte passed the newspaper clipping to Ella. "We're in the news!"

The afternoon passed with them enjoying their last few hours of being able to perform magic. They ate Rude Chips and Ever-Lasting Fruit Rolls; they pretended to not be in their particular carriage when excited students knocked, taking a page from Ace and Jude's book, standing on the threshold. And of course, they chatted about the amazing year and their adventure in the Dungeon of Unknown Doom...

Finally, the carriages slowed to a halt. They gathered their things and all of their possessions and got out to the station, where a sea of people were queuing to greet their children.

Charlotte ran to her uncle, who was grinning forcedly.

"Look who's here!" he said. Behind them, Charlotte recognized two faces from a photo her uncle had once shown her: Grannie Sarah and Grandpa Abram!

Grannie Sarah was stout, with a kind face and flyaway gray hair. She wore horn-rimmed glasses and a white blouse. Grandpa Abram was tall and balding, with deep eyes and glasses as well.

"And this *must* be Charlotte!" said Grannie Sarah. "Oh Charlotte, your eyes... they're Olivia's eyes..."

"Hello!" Charlotte called happily. Grandpa Abram beamed at her.

"So, this is our Charlotte," Grandpa Abram said, stepping forward to give her a hug. "Your eyes are just like your mother's."

Before Charlotte could reply to this, yet another person called out to her from across the platform.

"Charlotte!"

Charlotte turned to see Mrs. Ross bustling over to her, her arms laden with bags and trailing her two children behind her.

"Oh Charlotte, it's good to see you," Mrs. Ross hugged her. "Congratulations upon destroying the dungeon!"

Charlotte smiled.

"Congrats indeed!" piped in Grannie Sarah and Mrs. Snow at the same time.

"It is truly amazing," Oliver's father, Mr. Hayfield, said, shaking his head and coming over. "I can hardly believe it, such an achievement at your age!"

"They say you encountered Dagina?" inquired Mrs. Ross, looking very skeptical.

Ella nodded her head. The result was instant, Mrs. Ross cried out, Grannie Sarah and Grandpa Abram both gasped, and Mrs. Snow yelped

"No!"

"Twice," added Harry, obviously enjoying the effect.

The adults all shook their disbelievingly, looking very impressed.

"All these years we never came to see you," chortled Grandpa Abram. "Because we thought you'd be non-magical—well we were very wrong, weren't we? You're not only a witch, a mighty fine one at that."

"That doesn't even begin to cover these kids," Mr. Snow beamed at his son.

"Alas, should we leave?" prompted Grandpa Abram.

"We could," replied Charlotte. They walked out of the shop and wandered around in Hermes Plaza a bit before joining the large crowds to the pipe and away.

"Where do you live?" Charlotte asked Ella as they waited in line to get out of Hermes Plaza.

"There!" Ella said happily, pointing at a taupe colonial-style house near the border of the town. "Just ask around for the Ross home, they'll tell you. Visit anytime."

"Sure!"

They then met with Harry, Penelope, and Oliver. Then, they stepped into the pipe. After a moment's suffocation, they landed in the dusty bookshop.

"Okay, bye! Have a good summer, see you all soon!" Ella said, and managed to squeeze back in before someone came out.

"Bye guys!" said Harry, then went to board a train, flanked by his parents. "Keep in touch!"

"Bye, Charlotte, bye Penelope!" called Oliver as he and his mom walked off across the main hall.

"Now, look. We'll visit later. We have dinner with friends," said Grandpa Abram, giving Charlotte an affectionate hug.

"It's so good to finally meet you!" said Grannie Sarah. Then, they waved goodbye, touched a tin can, and disappeared.

"Alright, Penelope, Charlotte," Mr. Lexington said. "Let's all head home!" He called a taxi.

The moment her uncle unlocked the front door, several excited barks resounded in the hall. Before the door was even all the way open, a big mass of black fur bounded upon Charlotte, yapping excitedly and licking her ears.

"Jelly," Charlotte laughed, scratching his ears and finally calming him down. "I've missed you, too."

Charlotte finally managed to squeeze through the doorway, Jelly still running excitedly in circles all around her. Jelly's tail continued to wave in the air, so fast it was a blur. Charlotte sat down on the floor and patted Jelly all over, until he was finally satisfied. Then, Jelly turned to Penelope, judged her a moment, and licked her hand.

"He likes you," Charlotte laughed, entering the hall.

"I fed him every day at exactly 8 and 7," her uncle said. "I took her him for a walk every day at 5:30 and made sure his water bowl was full at all times. I took her him to the vet every three months and bathed him once a week and brushed his teeth and clipped his nails—!"

"He's looking great," Charlotte assured him.

They unloaded their trunks, and Charlotte and Penelope began redecorating. They had a good time clearing out half of Charlotte's closet and hanging up Penelope's clothes; Charlotte's room had one bare wall, which Penelope decorated with posters and keepsakes of her own; Charlotte cleared out her desk, which had accumulated a thick layer of dust over the semester, and reorganized it so that there'd be space for Penelope to work at; Charlotte also cleared out some of her dresser drawers so that Penelope could move her many possessions in. While they were laughing over a childhood photo Charlotte had unearthed during their deep-cleaning, Sofia simply materialized in front of them.

"Hey there," she said. "Sorry I wasn't there to greet you as you got off the train, I had a business meeting. Well, what can I say? Congratulations and good work, to all of you! I never could've expected that from you guys, and I'm proud of you all."

"Thanks!" Charlotte replied, blushing a little.

"Thank you, Sofia," Penelope also responded with a smile.

Charlotte glanced down at the photo in her hand and then back at Sofia. "Hey, Sofia, would you mind turning my bed into a bunk bed for us?" she asked, gesturing to the bed upon which she was sitting. "As you know, we haven't graduated, so we aren't allowed to do magic outside of school. But you've graduated already, so can you help?"

"No problem!" Sofia smiled warmly and flicked her wand twice. Charlotte's old bed disappeared, and a sturdy bunk bed appeared instead.

"Whoa!" Charlotte patted the mattress. She was now resting on the upper bunk. "Thanks a million, it's great!"

Charlotte hopped down from her perch. After a few greetings and questions, Sofia rolled back her right sleeve to check her watch and gave a start.

"It's been fifteen minutes!" she exclaimed. "I've got to get back to the office. I still have to deliver that report to old Royce in Department C before my break ends in five minutes, and sort out Stebbins's files before his meeting in ten. Well, see you later, sorry about this, I'll come around another time. Bye!"

They quickly said their goodbyes, and Sofia hurriedly disappeared into thin air.

"Back to cleaning, then," Charlotte grinned at Penelope. A moment later, they both burst into peals of laughter again at baby Charlotte in her diapers, brandishing a pencil in her chubby fist.

"You know," wheezed Penelope, when finally her breathing had returned to normal. "It looks like you're waving a wand. You were absolutely meant to be the great witch that you are."

Charlotte smiled wholesomely. "I guess so, I'm not sure about *great* though."

"Stop being modest," smiled Penelope.

"Yeah well, this is coming from the girl who I bet actually did brandish a wand at one."

That night, Charlotte couldn't sleep. She'd had a long, tiring day doing the cleanout, but nonetheless, as she lay upon her bottom bunk, staring up at the blue shadows the nightlight cast upon the ceiling, no drowsiness washed over her.

She rolled over onto her side. It was weird being back in her room. Quietly, she recalled her first year at Mountain View School of Magic from start to finish.

From the peculiar pigeon who broke her window to Professor Austin with her long white hair.

From the kind and diverse Rosses to the cozy abodes of Hermes Plaza.

From the light blue carriages to the homely halls, eccentric classes, and mysterious atmosphere of Mountain View.

From calm, wise, and venerable Professor Watonburn to her former archenemy, now sister, Penelope.

From her many peculiar lessons and assignments to the Dungeon of Unknown Doom.

From the five friends she'd made this year to the one dear friend she'd lost.

Charlotte felt it wasn't only her school that was different, but the person she was had changed too. She couldn't quite describe it, but it was a gut feeling, the same one that convinced her magic was real.

Contentedly, Charlotte exhaled deeply. After listening a moment to Penelope's slow breathing below her and the crickets chirping outside their window, she closed her eyes and fell immediately asleep.

The End

Acknowledgments

Thanks to Mrs. Kristin Pierce, a Gifted and Talented teacher in St. Vrain Valley School District in Erie, Colorado, who encouraged me. She devoted precious time to develop the quality of my book. Thank you for your contribution.

Thank you to my two best friends, Subikksha Kumar (aka Natasha) and Ryann Ambtman. Nat, thanks for all the fun times we had discussing books, etymology, and mythology. Ryann, thanks for all the time you talked with me about foils and other literary devices, and the great times we had discussing movie plotlines and characters. Both of you are the smartest, sharpest, yet kindest people I've met. Also, thank you to my other friends, Kate and Tayler, and all my classmates and fellow Harry Potter fans in the "campus campaign" to invite J.K. Rowling to come to our school, Black Rock Elementary.

Thank you to my elementary school principal, Mrs. O'Donnell; my fourth-grade teacher, Mrs. Cottle; and my school librarian, Mrs. Andres for their support in the J.K. Rowling "campaign."

Thank you to Tom and Margy. I stayed with you in your chalet many times and you made me familiar with the mountains. We hiked together to the Jurassic bathtubs, went snowshoeing in the winter, drove above the timberline in the summer, viewed the beautifully vibrant aspen leaves just before they fell, and stepped on rocks to cross brooks, after which my shoes were always soaked.

Also, thank you to Susanna Daniel for editing this book for me, and thank you to Ms. Kristin Mitchell for working on the graphic design and helping to make this book accessible to audiences.

And lastly, the thanks in the world to my mom and dad, who helped me tremendously in both the J.K. Rowling "campaign" and this publication. I couldn't have done this without your precious advice.

About the Author

Julia Gao is from Boulder, Colorado, she is a district Gifted and Talented student currently at middle school. She loves reading and is familiar with a wide range of fantasy books, fictional tropes, literary theory, Greek myths, and English etymology. She graduated from elementary school with a second place and a first place in the school Spelling Bee consecutively, and a US Presidential Award. Julia enjoys exploring the mysterious Rocky  Mountains of Colorado. In this book, she intertwines fantasy with local famous landmarks to create a gripping tale. She aspires for Stanford University for college and wants to be an astrophysicist.

CPSIA information can be obtained
at www.ICGtesting.com
Printed in the USA
JSHW082236210323
39269JS00004B/28